THE CAMP FIRE GIRLS

AT SCHOOL

BY

HILDEGARD G. FREY

The Camp Fire Girls at School

CHAPTER I.

CHRONICLES IN COLOR.

"Speaking of diaries," said Gladys Evans, "what do you think of this for one?" She spread out a bead band, about an inch and a half wide and a yard or more long, in which she had worked out in colors the main events of her summer's camping trip with the Winnebago Camp Fire Girls. The girls dropped their hand work and crowded around Gladys to get a better look at the band, which told so cleverly the story of their wonderful summer.

"Oh, look," cried "Sahwah" Brewster, excitedly pointing out the figures, "there's Shadow River and the canoe floating upside down, and Ed Roberts serenading Gladys—only it turned out to be Sherry serenading Nyoda—and the Hike, and the Fourth of July pageant, and everything!" The Winnebagos were loud in their expressions of admiration, and the "Don't you remembers" fell thick and fast as they recalled the events depicted in the bead band.

It was a crisp evening in October and the Winnebagos were having their Work Meeting at the Bradford house, as the guests of Dorothy Bradford, or "Hinpoha," as she was known in the Winnebago circle. Here were all the girls we left standing on the boat dock at Loon Lake, looking just the same as when we saw them last, a trifle less sunburned perhaps, but just as full of life and spirit. Scissors, needles and crochet hooks flew fast as the seven girls and their Guardian sat around the cheerful wood fire in the library. Sahwah was tatting, Gladys and Migwan were embroidering, and Miss Kent, familiarly known as "Nyoda," the Guardian of the Winnebago group, was "mending her hole-proof hose," as she laughingly expressed it. The three more quiet girls in the circle, Nakwisi the Star Maiden, Chapa the Chipmunk, and Medmangi the Medicine Man Girl, were working out their various symbols in crochet patterns. Hinpoha was down on the floor popping corn over the glowing logs and turning over a row of apples which had been set before the fireplace to warm. The firelight streaming over her red curls made them shine like burning embers, until it seemed as if some of the fire had escaped from the grate and was playing around her face. Every few minutes she reached out her hand and dealt a gentle slap on the nose of "Mr. Bob," a young cocker spaniel attached to the house of Bradford, who persistently tried to take the apples in his mouth. Nyoda finally came to the rescue and diverted his attention by giving him her darning egg to chew. The room was filled with the light-hearted chatter of the girls. Sahwah was relating with many giggles, how she had gotten into a scrape at school.

"And old Professor Fuzzytop made me bring all my books and sit up at that little table beside his desk for a week. Of course I didn't mind that a bit, because then I could see what everybody in the room was doing instead of just the few around me. The only thing I prayed for was that Miss Muggins wouldn't come in and see me, because she has taken a sort of fancy to me and makes it easy for me in Latin, but if I ever fall from grace she won't pass me. But of all the luck, right in the middle of the Fourth Hour when everybody was in the room studying, in she walked. I saw her as she opened the door and quick as a wink I opened up the big dictionary on the table and buried my nose in it, so she'd think I had gone up there of my own accord. She stopped and looked at me, then patted me encouragingly on the shoulder and remarked what a studious girl I was. I thought everybody in the room would die trying not to laugh, but nobody gave me away. She came in during the Fourth Hour for several days after that, and every time I flew to the sheltering arms of the dictionary, and she always made some approving remark out loud. Now she thinks I'm a shark and I have a better stand-in than ever with her. She told her Senior session room that there was a girl in the Junior room who was so keen after knowledge that no matter when she came into the room she always found her consulting the dictionary!"

Sahwah's imitation of the elderly and precise Miss Muggins was so close that the girls shrieked with laughter. Even Nyoda, who was a "faculty," and should have been the ally of the deluded instructor, was too much amused to say a word. "By the way, Sahwah," she said when the laughter had died down, "how are you coming on in Latin? The last time I saw you your Cicero had a strangle hold on you." Sahwah made a fearful grimace, and recited sarcastically:

"Not showers to larks more pleasing,

Not sunshine to the bee,

Not sleep to toil more easing,

Than Latin prose to me!

"The flocks shall leave the mountains,

The dew shall flee the rose,

The nymphs forsake the fountains,

Ere I forsake my prose!"

Nyoda laughed and shook her head at Sahwah, and "Migwan," otherwise Elsie Gardiner, looked up at the despiser of prose composition in mild wonderment. "I don't see how you can make such a fuss about learning Latin," she said, "it's the least of my troubles."

"But I'm not such a genius as you," answered Sahwah, "and my head won't stand the strain." Her mental limitations did not seem to cause her any anxiety, however, for she hummed a merry tune as she drew her tatting shuttle in and out.

Migwan leaned back in her chair and looked around the tastefully furnished room with quiet enjoyment. This library in the Bradford house was a never-ending delight to her. It was finished in dark oak and the walls were hung with a rich brown paper. The floor was polished and covered with oriental rugs, whose patterns she loved to trace. At one end of the room was a big fireplace and on each side of it a cozy seat, piled with tapestry covered cushions. Over the fireplace hung two slender swords, the property of some departed Bradford. The handsome chairs were upholstered in brown leather to match the other furnishings, and everything in the room, from the Italian marble Psyche on its pedestal in the corner to the softly glowing lamps, gave the impression of wealth and culture. Migwan contrasted it with the shabby sitting room in her own home and sighed. She was keenly responsive to beautiful surroundings and would have been happy to stay forever in this library. But beautiful as the furnishings were, they were the least part of the attraction. The real drawing card were the books that filled the cases on three sides of the room. There were books of every kind; fiction, poetry, history, travel, science; and whole sets of books in handsome bindings that Migwan fairly revelled in whenever she came to visit. Hinpoha herself was not fond of reading anything but fiction, and although she had the freedom of all the cases she never looked at anything but "story books." Before her parents went to Europe they had tried making her keep an average of one book of fiction to one of another kind in the hope of instilling into her a love for essays and history, but in the absence of her father and mother, history and essays were having a long vacation and fiction was working overtime.

"Let's play something," said Sahwah when the apples and popcorn had disappeared; "I'm tired of sitting still."

"Can't somebody please think of a new game?" said Hinpoha. "We've played everything we know until I'm sick of it."

"I thought of one the other day," said Gladys quietly. "I named it the 'Camp Fire Game.' You play it like Stage Coach, or Fruit Basket, only instead of taking parts of a coach or names of fruits you take articles that belong to the Camp Fire, like bead band, ring, moccasin, bracelet, fire, honor beads, symbol, fringe, Wohelo, hand sign, bow and drill, Mystic Fire, etc. Then somebody tells a story about Camp Fire Girls, and every time one of those articles is mentioned every one must get up and turn around. But if the words 'Ceremonial Meeting' or 'Council Fire' are mentioned, then all must change seats and the story teller tries to get a seat in the scramble, and the one who gets left out has to go on with the story."

"Good!" cried Nyoda, "let's play it. You tell the story first."

Gladys stood up in the center of the room and began: "Once upon a time there were a group of Camp Fire Girls called the Winnebagos, and they went to school in the Professors' big tepee on the avenue, where they pursued knowledge for all they were worth. So much wisdom did they imbibe that it was necessary to wear a head band to keep their heads from splitting open. Wherever they went they were immediately recognized by their rings and bracelets, and were pointed out as 'those dreadful young savages.' The professors and teachers hoped every day that they would not come to school, but they never stayed away because they received honor beads from their Guardian Mother for not being absent. Sometimes it seemed as if the tricks they did in class room could only have been accomplished by their having consulted one another, and yet it was impossible to catch them whispering in class because they always conversed by hand signs. However, this also led to disaster one day when one of our well-beloved sisters of the bow and drill tried to make the hand sign for 'girl,' and raised her hand above her head. The Big Chief, who was conducting the lesson, thought she wanted something, and said benevolently: 'What is your desire?' Absent-mindedly she replied, 'It is my desire to become a Camp Fire Girl and obey the Law of the Camp Fire, which is to seek beauty, give service, pursue knowledge, be trustworthy, hold on to health, glorify work, and be happy,' 'Begone,' said the Big Chief, 'what do you think this is, a Ceremonial Meeting?'"

At the words "Ceremonial Meeting" all the girls jumped up to change places, and in the scramble a vase was knocked off the table and broken. Every one sat rooted to the spot with fright, all except Mr. Bob, who fled at the sound of the crash as if he had been the guilty one. Hinpoha calmly collected the pieces and carried them out. "My mother will be extremely grateful to you for this when she comes home," she said. "If there was one vase in the house she hated it was this one. My Aunt Phoebe brought it from the World's Fair in Chicago and thinks it's the chief ornament of our home. Won't mother be glad when she finds it broken and she can prove that none of us did it?" The tension relaxed and the girls breathed easily again.

"When are your mother and father coming home?" asked Nyoda.

"They sailed last week on the Francona," answered Hinpoha.

"Weren't you worried to death to have them in Europe so long with the war going on?" asked Migwan.

"No, not much," said Hinpoha, "because they have been in Switzerland all the while, which is safe enough, and as they are coming home on a neutral vessel they have had no trouble getting passage. They should be here in a week." And Hinpoha's eyes shone with a great, glad light, for although she had been having the jolliest time imaginable, doing as she pleased in the house, which was in the care of easy-going "Aunt Grace," who never cared a bit what Hinpoha did so long as it did not bother her, she missed her mother sorely, and could hardly wait until she returned. Nyoda saw the transfigured look that came into her eyes when she spoke of her mother's home coming, and her own eyes went dim, for her mother had died when she was just Hinpoha's age.

After the breaking of the vase the game stopped and the girls sat down again in a quiet circle. "Do you know," said Nyoda, "that bead band Gladys made has given me an idea? Why can't we keep a personal record in bead work? It would be a great deal more interesting and picturesque than keeping a diary, and there would be no danger of your little sister getting hold of it and reading your secrets out loud to her friends."

"It's a great idea," said Migwan, who had always kept a diary and had suffered much from an inquisitive brother and sister.

"Besides," said Sahwah, "think how exciting it would be at Ceremonial Meetings, to sit with your life story hanging around your neck, and know that your neighbor was just breaking her neck trying to figure out what the little pictures meant. Wouldn't old Fuzzytop love to be able to read mine, though!" And Sahwah giggled extravagantly as she saw in her mind's eye the bead record of some of her activities in the Junior session room.

"Now, about all our activities," continued Nyoda, "are covered by the seven points of the Camp Fire Law, so that everything we do either fulfills or breaks the Law. What do you say if we register our commendable doings in colors, but record the event in black every time we break the Law?"

The girls thought this would be a fascinating game, and Sahwah remarked that she must send to the Outfitting Company for a bunch of black beads directly, as she had only a very few left.

"It's a good thing we didn't keep this record last summer," said Gladys with a thoughtful look in her eyes, "or mine would have been black from one end to the other."

"It wouldn't, either," said Sahwah vehemently. "You did more for us in the end than we ever did for you. And my sins were as scarlet as yours, every bit."

Since that terrible day in camp Gladys seemed to have been made over, and never once reverted to her old selfishness and superciliousness, so that she now had the love and esteem of every one of the Winnebagos. All mention of her old short-comings was quickly silenced by Sahwah, who now adored her, heart and soul. Gladys's entrance into the public school after two years at Miss Russell's had caused quite a stir among the girls of the neighborhood, who in times past had been wont to consider her proud and haughty, but her simple, unaffected manner quickly won for her a secure place in the affections of all. Teachers and scholars alike loved her.

Sahwah was still counting up her own misdemeanors at camp when the Evans's automobile came for Gladys, and reluctantly all the girls prepared to go home. It always seemed harder to break away from Hinpoha's house than from any of the others'. In spite of the rich furnishings it had a cozy, homey atmosphere of being used from one end to the other, and no guest, however humble, ever felt awkward or out of place there. Thus it usually happens that when people are entirely at ease in their own surroundings, they soon make others feel the same way too.

CHAPTER II.

A SUDDEN MISFORTUNE.

As the day drew near for the return of her mother and father Hinpoha went all over the house from garret to cellar seeing that everything was put to rights. She and the other Winnebagos took a trip into the country for bittersweet to decorate the fireplace in the library and in her father's study upstairs. With pardonable pride she arranged a little exhibition of the Craft work she had done in camp and the sketches she had made of the lake and hills. On the table in her mother's room she placed a work basket she had made of reed and lined with silk.

"Gracious sakes, child," said her aunt, from her rocking chair by the front window of the living-room, "what a fuss you are going to! One would think it was your Aunt Phoebe who was coming instead of your mother and father. They'll be just as glad to see you if the house isn't as neat as a pin from top to bottom." And Aunt Grace resumed her rocking and her novel, as unconcerned about the imminent return of the travelers as if it were nothing more than the daily visit of the milkman. Nothing short of an earthquake would ever shake Aunt Grace out of her settled complacency.

Hinpoha went happily on, seeing that every tack and screw was in place, and arranging the books in the cases to correspond to her father's catalog, for they had become sadly mixed during his absence. She even took out a volume of his favorite essays and pored over them diligently so that she might discuss them with him and show that she had used some of her time to good advantage. She straightened out her bureau drawers and mended all her clothes and stockings. When everything was in order she viewed the result with a happy feeling at the pleasure it would give her mother when she saw it. Hinpoha's most prominent trait in times past had not been neatness.

Nyoda, who had been called in to make a final inspection before Hinpoha was satisfied, wondered if all the girls were "seeking beauty" as earnestly as Hinpoha was. She envied Hinpoha the homecoming of her mother from the bottom of her heart. This feeling was particularly strong one afternoon as she sat in the school room after the close of school, looking over some English papers. It was the anniversary of the death of her mother and she sat recalling little incidents of her childhood before this best of chums had been taken away. As she sat there half dreaming she heard voices in the hall before her door.

"Have you heard the latest?" asked one voice.

"No," said the second voice, "what is it?"

"Why, the Francona has gone down," answered the first voice. "Struck a mine in the ocean."

At the word "Francona" Nyoda started up. That was the boat Hinpoha's parents were coming on! She hurried out into the hall after the two teachers. "What did you say about the Francona?" she asked. They handed her the "extra" they had been reading and she saw with her own eyes the account of the disaster. The list of "saved" was pitifully small, and Hinpoha's parents were not among them. Soon she came to the notation, "Among the lost are Mr. and Mrs. Adam Bradford, prominent Cleveland lawyer and his wife. Mr. Bradford was the son of the late Judge Bradford and a well-known man about town." Of what little avail is "prominence" when calamity stretches out her cruel hands! "Well known" and obscure gave up their lives together and found a grave side by side.

"You look like a ghost, Miss Kent," said one of the teachers. "Any friends of yours on board?"

"Dorothy Bradford's mother and father," answered Nyoda, "one of the pupils here at school."

Leaving her work unfinished, she hastened to Hinpoha's house. The news had just been learned there. Aunt Grace had fainted and was being revived with salts. Hinpoha flung herself on Nyoda and clung to her like a drowning person. Between neighbors and friends coming to sympathize and reporters from the newspapers seeking interviews the house was a pandemonium. Nyoda saw that Hinpoha would never quiet down in those surroundings and took her away to her own apartment. Of all the friends who offered consolation Nyoda was the one to whom Hinpoha turned for comfort. Here the brilliant young college woman and the simple girl were on a level, for they shared a common experience, and each could comprehend the other's sorrow.

Poor Hinpoha! She had need of all the consolation that Nyoda could give her in the days that followed. Full of bitterness as her cup was, there was to be added yet one more drop—the drop that caused it to run over. Aunt Phoebe came to live with her and be the mistress of the Bradford house. At some time in the past Judge Bradford and his sister Phoebe had been named joint guardians of Hinpoha, but the Judge was now dead and Aunt Phoebe was the sole guardian. Aunt Phoebe was a spinster of the type usually described in books, tall and spare, with steely blue eyes. She was sixty years old, but she might have been a hundred and sixty, for all the sympathy she had with youth. She had been disappointed in love when she was twenty and had never thought kindly of any man since. From her earliest childhood Hinpoha had dreaded the very name of Aunt Phoebe. When she came to visit a restraint fell over the whole house. The usual lively chatter at the dinner table was hushed, and Aunt Phoebe held forth in solemn tones, generally berating some unfortunate person who nearly always happened to be a good friend of Mrs. Bradford's. Hinpoha would be called up for a minute examination of her clothes and manners and would invariably do something which was not right in her great aunt's eyes.

She had a vivid recollection of going tobogganing down the long front walk one winter day, her jolly mother on the sled with her, steering it adroitly around the corner and up the sidewalk for a distance after leaving the slope. Such fun they were having that they did not look to see if the road was clear, and went bumping into a female figure that was coming majestically along the street, knocking her off her feet and into a snowdrift. It was Aunt Phoebe, coming to make a formal afternoon call. She sat bolt upright in the snow and adjusted her lorgnette to see if by any chance her grandniece could be one of those rowdy children. When she discovered that it was not only Hinpoha, but her mother as well, frolicking so indecorously, she was speechless. Mrs. Bradford started to make an abject apology, but the sight of Aunt Phoebe sitting in the snowdrift with her lorgnette was too much for her and she went off into a peal of laughter, in which Hinpoha joined gleefully. It was weeks before Aunt Phoebe could be coaxed to make another visit. And this was the woman who was coming to take the place of Hinpoha's beloved mother!

Aunt Grace left the day she came. There was not enough room in one house for her and Aunt Phoebe. With Aunt Phoebe came "Silky," a wiggling, snapping Skye terrier. He gave one glance at genial Mr. Bob, who was rolling on his back before the fireplace, and with a growl fastened his teeth into his neck. Hinpoha rescued her pet and bore him away to her room, where she shed tears of despair while he licked her hand sympathetically. Aunt Phoebe's first act was to put Hinpoha into deep mourning. Hinpoha objected strenuously, but there was no help, and she went to school swathed from head to foot in black. Nyoda was wrathful at the sight, for if there was one point she felt strongly about it was putting children into mourning. Among the gaily dressed girls Hinpoha stood out like some dark spirit from the underworld, casting a gloom wherever she went.

"Where is that beautiful vase I brought your mother from the World's

Fair?" asked Aunt Phoebe one day, suddenly missing it.

"It was accidently broken at our last Camp Fire meeting," answered Hinpoha, with a tightening around her heart when she thought of that last happy gathering.

"Camp Fire!" said Aunt Phoebe with a snort. "You don't mean to tell me that you are mixed up in any such foolishness as that?"

"I certainly am," said Hinpoha energetically, "and it isn't foolishness, either. I've learned more since I have been a Camp Fire Girl than I did in all the years before."

"Well, you may consider yourself graduated, then," said Aunt Phoebe, drily, "for I'll have no such nonsense about me. I can teach you all you need to know outside of what you learn in school."

"Camp Fire always had mother's fullest approval," said Hinpoha darkly.

"I dare say," returned her aunt. "But I want you to understand once for all that I won't have any girls holding 'meetings' here, to upset the house and break valuable ornaments."

"But you don't care if I go to them at other girls' houses, do you?" asked Hinpoha, the fear gripping her that she was to be denied the consolation of these weekly gatherings with the Winnebagos.

"I don't want you to have anything to do with that Camp Fire business," said Aunt Phoebe in a tone of finality, and Hinpoha left the room, her heart swelling with bitterness. She was too wise to argue the point with Aunt Phoebe, and resolved to depend on Nyoda to show her the way. She dried her tears and went down to the living room and began to play softly on the piano. It had been her mother's piano, the wedding gift of her father, and it seemed that her mother's spirit hovered over it. It was the first time she had touched the keys since that awful Wednesday when the world had been turned into chaos; she had had no heart to play, but to-day the sound of the music comforted her and her bitter resentment against her aunt lost some of its sting. She played on, lost in memories, when suddenly the sharp voice of her aunt brought her back to earth. "What does this mean?" cried Aunt Phoebe, "playing on the piano when your father and mother have just died! I never heard of such a thing! Come away immediately and don't open that piano again until our period of mourning is over." She closed the piano and locked it, putting the key into her bag.

Under Aunt Phoebe's management the house soon lost its look of inviting friendliness. The blinds were always kept drawn, so that even on the brightest days the rooms had a gloomy appearance. No more cheerful wood fires crackled and glowed in the grate. They made ashes on the rugs and were extravagant, as the house was heated by steam. The bookcases were locked and Hinpoha was forbidden to read fiction, as this was not proper when one was in mourning. "You will become acquainted with much pleasant literature reading to me while I crochet," she said when Hinpoha rose in revolt at this edict. The "pleasant literature" which Aunt Phoebe was just then perusing was a History of the Presbyterian Church in eleven volumes, which bored Hinpoha so it nearly gagged her.

Besides, Aunt Phoebe constantly found fault with Hinpoha's manner of reading. It was either too loud or not loud enough; either too fast or too slow, but it was never right. That reading aloud was the last straw to Hinpoha. After sitting still a whole afternoon getting her school lessons, she longed to move about after supper, but then Aunt Phoebe expected her to sit still the entire evening and entertain her with the activities of the Early Presbytery. After nearly a week of this deadly dullness Hinpoha was ready to fly. And yet Aunt Phoebe was not conscious that there was anything wrong in the way she was treating Hinpoha. She cared for her in her frozen way. She was merely trying to bring her up in the way she herself had been brought up by a maiden aunt, not taking into account that this was another day and age. In her time it was considered the proper thing to shut down on all lightheartedness after a death in the family, and she was adhering steadfastly to the old principles. She was yet to learn that she could not force obsolete customs upon a girl who had lived for sixteen years in the sunlight of modern ideas.

All Hinpoha's troubles were confided to Nyoda, who sympathized with her entirely, but bade her be of good cheer and hope for the time when Aunt Phoebe would see for herself that the new way was best; and above all to win the respect and liking of her aunt the first thing, as more could be accomplished in this way than by being antagonistic. "I don't suppose you could go for a long walk with me Sunday afternoon?" said Nyoda.

Hinpoha shook her head sadly. "We don't do anything like that on Sunday," she answered, with resentment flaming in her eye. "We go to church morning and evening and in the afternoon I am supposed to read the Bible or a book by a man named Thomas à Kempis." Nyoda turned her eyes inward with such a comical expression that Hinpoha forgot her troubles for a moment and laughed.

"The Bible and Thomas à Kempis," said Nyoda musingly; "where did I hear those two mentioned before? Oh, I have it! Did you ever read this anywhere, 'Commit to memory one hundred verses of the Bible or an equal amount of sacred literature, such as Thomas à Kempis'?"

Hinpoha hung her head, still smiling. "Why, Nyoda," she said, "there's a chance to earn an honor bead that I probably wouldn't have thought of otherwise!"

"Right-o," said Nyoda. "'It's an ill wind,' you know. And while you are doing so much Bible reading you will undoubtedly come across something about 'in the wilderness a cedar,' and will learn that most waste places can be turned into blooming gardens if we only know how."

"Thank you," said Hinpoha, "I always feel less forlorn after a talk with you." Her face brightened, but immediately fell again. "But what good will it do me to work for honors?" she said sadly. "Aunt Phoebe won't let me come to the meetings."

"Won't she really?" asked Nyoda in surprise. Hinpoha nodded, near to tears. "I must see about that," said Nyoda resolutely. "I think if I explain the mission and activities of Camp Fire she will not object to your belonging. She probably has a wrong idea of what it means."

Accordingly Nyoda came a-calling on Aunt Phoebe that very night. In addition to being very pretty Nyoda had a great deal of dignity, and when she put on her formal manner she looked very impressive indeed. She did not act as if she had come to see Hinpoha at all, but asked for "Miss Bradford," and said she had come to pay her respects to her new neighbor. She listened politely to Aunt Phoebe's account of her last siege of rheumatism, admired her crochet work, and hoped she liked this street as well as her former neighborhood. She said she had often seen Miss Bradford's name in the papers in connection with various charitable organizations and was very glad to have the honor of meeting the sister of the prominent Judge. Aunt Phoebe was pleased and flattered at the deference paid her. But when Nyoda announced herself as the leader of the club to which Hinpoha belonged and asked permission for her to attend the meetings, she refused. She was perfectly polite about it, and did not mention her antipathy to Camp Fire, and taking refuge behind her favorite excuse, that of being in mourning, stated that she did not wish Hinpoha to go out in society.

"But this isn't 'society'," broke in Hinpoha desperately.

"A meeting of a club partakes of a social nature," returned her aunt, "and is not to be thought of." And there the matter rested.

So Nyoda had to depart without accomplishing her mission. Hinpoha, utterly crushed, followed her to the door, and Nyoda gave her hand a reassuring squeeze. "Don't despair, dear," she whispered hopefully; "she will come around to it eventually, but it will take time. Be patient. And in the meantime read this," and she slipped into her hand a tiny copy of "The Desert of Waiting." "Just be true to the Law, and see if you cannot find the roses among the thorns and from them distil the precious ointment that will open the door of the City of Your Desire later on."

Hinpoha thrust the little book into her blouse, and when she was safe in her own room read it from cover to cover. When she finished there was a song in her heart again and a light in her eyes. Resolutely she turned her face to the East and began her long sojourn in the Desert of Waiting.

Nyoda pondered the problem for a long while that night, and the next day she went to call on Gladys's mother. Mrs. Evans had taken a great liking to the popular young teacher of whom Gladys was so fond, and cordially invited her to spend as much time as she could at the house with the family. It was to her, then, that Nyoda appealed for advice in regard to Hinpoha. Mrs. Evans made a slight grimace when the facts were laid before her.

"If that isn't just like Phoebe Bradford," she exclaimed indignantly. "Trying to shut up that poor girl like a nun to conform to some moth-eaten ideas of hers! If the Judge were alive that house wouldn't look as if there was a perpetual funeral going on! I certainly will call and see if I can do anything to change her mind, although I doubt very much if that could be accomplished by human means."

The next day Aunt Phoebe was agreeably surprised to receive a call from Mrs. Evans, "All the best people in the neighborhood are making haste to call on the sister of Judge Bradford," she reflected complacently. Mrs. Evans made herself very agreeable, speaking of many friends they had in common, and finally led the conversation around to Hinpoha.

"The child looks very pale," she said. "I presume the death of her parents was a terrible shock to her?"

Aunt Phoebe dabbed her eyes with her black-bordered handkerchief. "The hand of misfortune has fallen heavily upon this house," she said mournfully.

"It has indeed!" thought Mrs. Evans. Aloud she said, "You must not let the girl grieve herself sick. Cheerful company is what she needs at this time. Make her go out with the Camp Fire Girls as much as possible."

Aunt Phoebe drew herself up rather stiffly. "I do not approve of the

Camp Fire Girls," she said.

"Not approve of the Camp Fire Girls!" echoed Mrs. Evans in well-feigned astonishment; "why, what's wrong with them?"

Just what the great objection was Aunt Phoebe was not prepared to say, but she remarked that such nonsense had never been thought of in her day. "And, of course," she added, hiding behind her usual argument, "while we are in mourning my grandniece will not go out to any gatherings."

"Why, I wouldn't think of keeping Gladys home for that reason," said Mrs. Evans, seeing the subterfuge. "She went to a Camp Fire meeting the day after her grandfather's funeral. It's not like going to a social function, you know."

Aunt Phoebe shook her head, but her policy of seclusion for Hinpoha was getting shaky. Mrs. Homer Evans was a power in the community, and what she did set the fashion in a good many directions. Aunt Phoebe was very anxious to keep her as a permanent acquaintance, and if Mrs. Evans gave her sanction to this Camp Fire business, she wondered if she had not better swallow her prejudice—outwardly at least, for she declared inwardly that she had never heard of such foolishness in all her born days. When Mrs. Evans went home Aunt Phoebe had actually promised that after three months Hinpoha might attend the meetings as before. Those three months of mourning, however, were sacred to her, and on no account would she have consented to allow a single ray of cheer to enter the house during that period.

CHAPTER III.

SOME TRIALS OF GENIUS.

"The sum of the angles of a triangle is equal to two right angles." Migwan drew the construction lines as indicated in the book and labored valiantly to understand why the Angle A was equal to its alternate, DBA, her brow puckered into a studious frown. Geometry was not her long suit, her talents running to literature and languages. Outside the October sun was shining on the crimson and yellow maples, making the long street a scene of dazzling splendor. The carpet of dry leaves on the walk and sidewalk tantalized Migwan with their crisp dryness; she longed to be out swishing and crackling through them. She sighed and stirred impatiently in her chair, wishing heartily that Euclid had died in his cradle.

"I can't study with all this noise going on!" she groaned, flinging her pencil and compass down in despair. Indeed, it would have taken a much more keenly interested person than Migwan to have concentrated on a geometry lesson just then. From somewhere upstairs there came an ear-splitting din. It sounded like an earthquake in a tin shop, mingled with the noise of the sky falling on a glass roof, and accompanied by the tramping of an army; a noise such as could only have been produced by an extremely large elephant or an extremely small boy amusing himself indoors. Migwan rose resolutely and mounted the stairs to the room overhead, where her twelve-year-old brother and two of his bosom friends were holding forth. "Tom," she said appealingly, "wouldn't you and the boys just as soon play outdoors or in somebody else's house? I simply can't study with all that noise going on."

"But the others have no punching bag," said Tom in an injured tone, "and

Jim brought George over especially to-day to practice."

"Can't you take the punching bag over to Jim's?" suggested Migwan desperately.

"Sure," said Jim good-naturedly; "that's a good idea." So the boys unscrewed the object of attraction and departed with it, their pockets bulging with ginger cookies which Migwan gave them as a reward for their trouble. Silence fell on the house and Migwan returned to the mastering of the sum of the angles. Geometry was the bane of her existence and she was only cheered into digging away at it by the thought of the money lying in her name in the bank, which she had received for giving the clew leading to little Raymond Bartlett's discovery the summer before, and which would pay her way to college for one year at least.

The theorem was learned at last so that she could make a recitation on it, even if she did not understand it perfectly, and Migwan left it to take up a piece of work which gave her as much pleasure as the other did pain. This was the writing of a story which she intended to send away to a magazine. She wrote it in the back of an old notebook, and when she was not working at it she kept it carefully in the bottom of her shirtwaist box, where the prying eyes of her younger sister would not find it. She had all the golden dreams and aspirations of a young authoress writing her first story, and her days were filled with a secret delight when she thought of the riches that would soon be hers when the story was accepted, as it of course would be. If she had known then of the long years of cruel disillusionment that would drag their weary length along until her efforts were finally crowned with success it is doubtful whether she would have stayed in out of the October sunshine so cheerfully and worked with such enthusiasm.

Migwan's family could have used to advantage all the gold which she was dreaming of earning. After her father died her mother's income, from various sources, amounted to only about seventy-five dollars a month, which is not a great amount when there are three children to keep in school, and it was a struggle all the way around to make both ends meet. Mrs. Gardiner was a poor manager and kept no accounts, and so took no notice of the small leaks that drained her purse from month to month. She was fond of reading, as Migwan was, and sat up until midnight every night burning gas. Then the next morning she would be too tired to get up in time to get the children off to school, and they would depart with a hasty bite, according to their own fancy, or without any breakfast at all, if they were late. She bought ready-made clothes when she could have made them herself at half the cost, and generally chose light colors which soiled quickly. She never went to the store herself, depending on Tom or scatter-brained Betty, her younger daughter, to do her marketing, and in consequence paid the highest prices for inferior-grade goods.

Thus the seventy-five dollars covered less ground every month as prices mounted, and little bills began to be left outstanding. Part of the income was from a house which rented for twenty dollars but this last month the tenants had abruptly moved, and that much was cut off. Migwan, unbusiness-like as she was, began to be worried about the condition of their affairs, and worked on her story feverishly, that it might be turned into money as soon as possible. She was deep in the intricacies of literary construction when her mother entered the room, broom in hand and dust cap on head, and sank into a chair.

"Do you suppose you could finish this sweeping?" she asked Migwan. "My back aches so I just can't stand up any longer."

"Why can't Betty do it?" asked Migwan a little impatiently, for she thought she ought not be disturbed when she was engaged in such an important piece of work.

"Betty's off in the neighborhood somewhere," said her mother wearily. "Did you ever see her around when there was any work to be done?" Migwan was filled with exasperation. That was the way things always went at their house. Tom was allowed to upset the place from one end to the other without ever having to pick up his things; Betty was never asked to do any housework, and her mother left the Saturday dinner dishes standing and began to sweep in the afternoon and then was unable to finish. Migwan was just about to suggest a search for the errant Betty, when she remembered the "Give Service" part of the Camp Fire Law. She rose cheerfully and took the broom from her mother's hand.

"Lie down a while, mother," she said, plumping up the pillows on the couch. Mrs. Gardiner sank down gratefully and Migwan put away her story and went at the sweeping. She soon turned it into a game in which she was a good fairy fighting the hosts of the goblin Dust, and must have them completely vanquished by four o'clock, or her magic wand, which had for the time being taken the shape of a broom, would vanish and leave her weaponless. Needless to say, she was in complete possession of the field when the clock struck the charmed hour. Being then out of the mood to continue her writing, she passed on into the kitchen and attacked the Fortress of Dishes, which she razed to the ground completely, leaving her banner, in the form of the dish towel, flying over the spot.

"What are you planning for supper?" she asked her mother, looking into the sitting room to see how she was feeling.

"Oh, dear, I don't know," said Mrs. Gardiner. "I hadn't given it a thought. I don't believe there's anything left from dinner. Run down to the store, will you, and get a couple of porterhouse steaks, there's a dear. And stop at the baker's as you come by and get us each a cream puff for dessert. Betty is so fond of them." Migwan returned to the kitchen and got her mother's pocketbook. There was just twenty-five cents in it. Migwan realized with a shock that it would not pay for what her mother wanted, and her sensitive nature shrank from asking to have things charged.

"I won't buy the cream puffs," she decided. "I wonder if there is anything in the house I could make into a dessert?" Search revealed nothing but a bag of prunes, which had been on the shelf for months, and were as dry as a bone. They did not appeal to Migwan in the least, but there was nothing else in evidence. "I might make prune whip," she thought rather doubtfully. "They're pretty hard, but I can soak them. I'll need the oven to make prune whip, so I will bake the potatoes too." She hunted around for the potatoes and finally found them in a small paper bag. "Buying potatoes two quarts at a time must be rather expensive," she reflected. She put the prunes to soak and the potatoes in the oven and went down to the store. "How much is porterhouse steak?" she asked before she had the butcher cut any off.

"Twenty-eight cents a pound," answered the man behind the counter.

Migwan gave a little gasp. The money she had would not even buy a pound.

"How much is round steak?" she inquired.

"Twenty-two," came the reply.

"Give me twenty-five cents' worth," she said. It did not look particularly tender and Migwan thought distressedly how her mother would complain when she found round steak instead of porterhouse. "But there is no help for it," she said to herself grimly, "beggars cannot be choosers." She stopped on the way home to get the recipe for prune whip from Sahwah. Sahwah was not at home, but her mother gave Migwan the recipe and added many directions as to the proper mixing of the ingredients. "Is—is there any way of making tough round steak tender?" she asked timidly, just a little ashamed to admit that they had to eat round steak.

"There certainly is," answered Mrs. Brewster. "You just pound all the flour into it that it will take up. I hardly ever buy porterhouse steaks any more since I learned that trick. I am having some to-night. It is one of our favorite dishes here. Round steak prepared in this way is known in the restaurants as 'Dutch steak,' and commands a high price." Considerably cheered by this last intelligence, Migwan sped home and got her prune dessert into the oven and then set to work transforming the tough steak into a tender morsel.

"What kind of meat is this?" asked her mother when they had taken their places at the table.

"Guess," said Migwan.

"It tastes like tenderloin," said her mother.

"Guess again," said Migwan gleefully; "it's round steak."

"The butcher must be buying better meat than usual, then," said Mrs.

Gardiner. "I never got such round steak as this out here before."

"And you never will, either," said Migwan, swelling with pride, "if you leave it to the butcher," and she told how she had treated the steak to produce the present result.

"I never heard of that before," said her mother, amazed at this simple culinary trick.

Next the prune whip was brought on and pronounced good by every one and "bully" by Tom, who ate his in great spoonfuls. "I see I'll have to let you get the meals after this," said Mrs. Gardiner to Migwan. "You have a knack of putting things together, which I have not."

Migwan was too tired to write any more that night after the dishes were done, but she was entirely light-hearted as she wove into her bead band the symbols of that day's achievements—a broom and a frying pan. She had learned something that afternoon besides how to prepare beefsteak. She had waked up to the careless fashion in which the house was being run, and her head was full of plans for cutting down expenses. Monday afternoon, on her way home from school, Migwan saw a farmer's wagon standing in front of the Brewsters' home, and Mrs. Brewster stood at the curb, buying her winter supply of potatoes.

"Have you put your potatoes in yet?" she asked as Migwan came along.

Migwan stopped. "I don't believe we ever bought them in large quantities," she answered. "How much are they a bushel?"

"Sixty-five cents," said the farmer. Migwan made a quick mental calculation. At the rate they had been buying potatoes in two-quart lots they had been paying a dollar and seventy-five cents a bushel. Migwan came to a sudden decision.

"Are they all good?" she asked Mrs. Brewster.

"They have always been in the past years," answered Sahwah's mother, "and I have bought my potatoes from this man for the last six winters."

"How many would it take for a family of four?" asked Migwan.

"About five bushels," answered Mrs. Brewster.

"All right," said Migwan to the man; "bring five bushels over to this address." The potatoes were duly deposited in the Gardiner cellar, without asking the advice of Mrs. Gardiner, which was the only safe way of getting things done, for had she been consulted she would surely have wanted to wait a while, and then would have kept putting it off until it was too late. It was the same way with flour and sugar. Migwan found that her mother had been buying these in small quantities at an exorbitant price, and calmly took matters into her own hands, ordering a whole barrel of flour, because there was more in a barrel even than in four sacks. A certain large store was offering a liberal discount that week on fifty pounds of sugar, and Migwan took advantage of this sale also.

Then she had a terrified counting up. Those three items, potatoes, flour and sugar, had used up every cent of that week's income, leaving nothing at all for running expenses. All other supplies would have to be bought on credit. Migwan made a careful estimate of the necessary expenses for the coming week, and pare down as she might, the sum was nearly fifteen dollars. The loss of the rent money was making itself keenly felt. "Mother," she said quietly, looking up from her account book, "we can't live on fifty-five dollars a month. We must rent the house again immediately."

Mrs. Gardiner made a gesture of despair. "The sign has been up nearly a month, and if people don't make inquiries I can't help it."

"Have you been in the house since the last people moved out?" asked

Migwan.

"No," said Mrs. Gardiner; "what good would that do? I haven't the time to go all the way over to the East Side to look at that old house. People know it's for rent, and if they want it they'll take it without my sitting over there waiting for them."

Nevertheless, Migwan made the long trip the very next day after school to look at the property. "It's no wonder no one has been making inquiries for it," she said when she returned. "The 'For Rent' sign was gone and I found it later when I was going back up the street. Some boys had used it to make the end piece of a wagon. Then, the plumbing is bad and the cellar is flooded, and the water will not run off in the kitchen sink. These must have been the repairs the old tenants wanted made when you told them you had no money to fix the house, and so they moved. I don't blame them at all.

"Then, there is another thing I thought of when I was looking through the rooms. You know that big unfinished space over the kitchen? Well, I thought, why can't we make a furnished room of that? There is space enough to build a large room and a bathroom, for part of it is just above the bathroom downstairs. A large furnished room with a private bath would bring in ten dollars a month. It is just at the head of the back stairs and the side door where the back stairs connect with the cellar way could be used as a private entrance, so the tenants of the house would not be disturbed in the least. It would cost over a hundred dollars to do it, most likely, but we could borrow the money from my college fund and the extra rent would soon pay it back." Migwan's eyes were shining with ambition.

Mrs. Gardiner shook her head wearily. "We never could do it," she answered. "Something would surely happen to upset our plans."

But Migwan was not to be waved aside. She had seen a vision of increased income and meant to make it come true. She argued the merits of her idea until Mrs. Gardiner was too tired of the subject to argue back, and agreed that if Miss Kent approved the step she would give her consent. Nyoda was therefore called into consultation. She looked at the house and saw no reason why the improvements could not be made to advantage. The house was in a good neighborhood, and furnished rooms were always in demand. She advised the step and gave Mrs. Gardiner the names of several contractors whom she knew to be reliable. Mrs. Gardiner was a little breathless at the speed with which things were moving, but there was no stopping Migwan once she was started. A contractor was engaged and work begun on the house one week from the day Migwan had thought of the plan.

Meanwhile financial matters at home were in bad shape, and Mrs. Gardiner willingly gave over the distribution of the family budget to Migwan. She herself was utterly unable to cope with the problem. And Migwan surprised even herself by the efficient way in which she managed things. By planning menus with the greatest care and omitting meat from the bill of fare to a great extent she made it possible to live on their slender income until the rent would begin to come in again.

"Whatever have you done with yourself?" asked Gladys at the weekly meeting of the Camp Fire. "Of late you rush home from school as if you were pursued." Migwan only laughed and said she had had uncommonly hard problems to solve these last few weeks. The other girls of course did not know the exact state of the Gardiner finances, and never dreamed that Migwan was having a struggle even to stay in high school. She was such a fine, aristocratic-looking girl, and was so sparkling and witty all the time that it was hard to connect her with poverty and worry.

"Let's all go to the matinee next Saturday afternoon," suggested Gladys. "The 'Blue Bird' is going to be played." The girls agreed eagerly and asked Gladys to get seats for them, all but Migwan, who said nothing.

"Don't you want to go, Migwan?" they asked.

"Not this time," Migwan answered in a casual tone. "There is something else I have to do Saturday afternoon." The girls accepted this explanation readily. It never occurred to them that Migwan could not afford to go.

"What is this mysterious something you are always doing?" asked Gladys teasingly. "Girls, I believe Migwan is writing a book. She has retired from polite society altogether." Migwan smiled blandly at her, but made no answer.

At home that night, however, she felt very low-spirited indeed. She was only human, after all, and wanted dreadfully to go to the matinee with the girls. Gladys would take them all to Schiller's afterward for a parfait and bring them home in style in her machine. It did not seem fair that she should be cut off from every pleasure that involved the spending of a little money. This was her last year in high school, the year which should be the happiest, but she must resolutely turn her face away from all those little festivities that add such touches of color to the memory fabric of school days. She knew that at the merest hint of her circumstances to Gladys or Nyoda they would have gladly paid her way everywhere the group went, but Migwan's pride forbade this. If she could not afford to go to places she would stay at home and nobody would be any the wiser. Nevertheless, a few tears would come at the thought of the good time she was missing, and she had no heart to work on her story.

"Cry-baby!" she said to herself fiercely, winking the tears back. "Crying because you can't do as you would like all the time! You're lots better off than poor Hinpoha this very minute, even if she is rich. You ought to be ashamed of yourself!" The thought of Hinpoha, who would likewise miss the jolly party, comforted her somewhat, and she dried her tears and fell to writing with a will.

Now Nyoda, although she did not know just how hard pressed the Gardiners were at that time, rather surmised something of the kind, and wondered, after she left the girls, if that were not the reason for Migwan's not planning to go to the matinee. She remembered Migwan's saying some time before that she wanted very much to see "The Bluebird" when it came. She knew it would never do to offer to pay Migwan's way; Migwan was too proud for that. She lay awake a long time over it and finally formulated a plan. The next morning when Migwan came to school she saw a conspicuous notice on the Bulletin Board:

LOST: Handbag containing book of lecture notes and ticket for Saturday afternoon's performance of "The Bluebird." Finder may keep theater ticket if he or she will return notebook to Miss Moore, Room 10.

Migwan read the notice and passed on, as did the other pupils. That morning in English class Nyoda sent Migwan to an unused lecture room to get an English book she had left there. When Migwan opened the door she stumbled over something on the floor. It was a lady's handbag. She opened it and found Miss Moore's notebook and the theater ticket inside. Miss Moore was overjoyed at the return of the notebook and insisted on her keeping the ticket, which Migwan at first declined to accept. "My dear child," said Miss Moore, "if you knew what trouble I had collecting those notes you would think, too, that it was worth the price of a theater ticket to get them back!" And when Migwan's back was turned she winked solemnly at Nyoda. By a curious coincidence that seat was directly behind those occupied by the other Winnebagos!

CHAPTER IV.

ANOTHER KITCHEN.

The night of the last Camp Fire Meeting Gladys and Nyoda might have been seen in close consultation. "The first pleasant Saturday," said Nyoda.

"Remember, it's my treat," said Gladys.

The first week in November was as balmy as May, with every promise of fine weather on Saturday. Accordingly, Nyoda gathered all the Winnebagos around her desk on Thursday and made an announcement. Sahwah forgot that she was in a class room and started to raise a joyful whoop, but Nyoda stifled it in time by putting her hand over her mouth. "I can't help it!" cried Sahwah; "we're going on a trip up the river! I'm going to paddle the Keewaydin once more!"

The plan suggested by Gladys and just announced by Nyoda was this: The following Saturday they would charter a launch big enough to hold them all, and follow the course of the Cuyahoga River upstream to the dam at the falls, where they would land and cook their dinner over an open fire. They would tow the Keewaydin, Sahwah's birchbark canoe, behind the launch, and some time during the day would manage to let every one go for a paddle. The Winnebagos thrilled with pleasurable anticipation, all but Hinpoha, who crept sadly away, for she could not bear to hear about the fun that was being planned when she could not have a part in it.

One desire of her heart was being fulfilled, and she was getting thin. What a whole summer of rigid dieting had not been able to accomplish was brought to pass by a few weeks of mental suffering, and her clothes were beginning to hang on her. Her appetite began to fail her, and her aunt, noticing this, bought her a big bottle of tonic, which, taken before meals, killed any small desire for food she may have had. Then Aunt Phoebe decided that the two-mile walk to school was too much for her, and had her taken and called for in the machine, much to Hinpoha's disgust, for that walk was her chief joy these days. After a week of the tonic her soul rebelled against the nauseous dose, and when the first bottle was empty and Aunt Phoebe sent her to get it refilled, she "refilled" it herself with a mixture of licorice candy and water, which produced a black syrup similar in appearance to the original medicine, but minus the bad taste and the stigma of "patent medicine," a thing which the Winnebagos had promised their Guardian they would not take. As this was deceiving her aunt she felt obliged to put a blot on her head 'scutcheon, in the form of a black record, but she was so inwardly amused at it that her appetite improved of its own accord, and Aunt Phoebe remarked in a gratified way that she had never known the equal of Mullin's Modifier as a tonic.

Migwan finished her story, copied it carefully on foolscap and sent it away to a magazine, confident that in a very short time she would behold it in print, and the payment she would receive for it would keep her in spending money throughout the school year. So with a light and merry heart she set out for Gladys's house on Saturday morning, where the girls were all to meet for the outing. It was one of those dream-like days in late autumn, when the earth, still decked in her brilliant garments, seems to lie spellbound in the sunshine, as if there were no such thing as the coming of winter.

The girls, clad in blue skirts and white middies and heavy sweaters, were whirled down to the dock in the Evans's automobile, with the Keewaydin tied upright at the back. The launch was waiting for them, at one of the big boat docks, sandwiched in between two immense lake steamers. Nothing could have been a greater contrast to their trip up the Shadow River the summer before than this excursion. On that other trip they had been the only living beings on the horizon, and nature was supreme everywhere, but here they were fairly engulfed by the works of man. The tiny craft nosed her way among giant steamers, six-hundred-foot freighters, coal barges, lighters, fire boats, tugs, scows, and all the other kinds of vessels that crowd the river-harbor of a great lake port. Viewed from below, the steel structure of the viaduct over the river stretched out like the monstrous skeleton of some prehistoric beast. Whistles shrieked deafeningly in their ears and trains pounded jarringly over railroad bridges. A jack-knife bridge began to descend over their very heads. Over where the new bridge was being constructed men stood on slender girders high in the air, catching red-hot rivets that were being tossed them, while an automatic riveting hammer filled the air with its nerve-destroying clamor. Everywhere was bustle and confusion, and noise, noise, noise.

And in the midst of this tumult the tiny launch, filled with laughing girls, threaded its way up the black river, flying the Winnebago banner, while behind it trailed a birchbark canoe, with Sahwah squatting calmly in the stern, leaning her back against her paddle. Many times they had to bury their noses in their handkerchiefs to shut out the smells that assailed them on every side. On they chugged, past the lumber yards with their acres of stacked boards, some of which had come from the very neighborhood of Camp Winnebago; past the chemical works, pouring out its darkly polluted streams into the river. "Ugh," said Gladys with a shiver, "to think that that stuff flows on into the lake and we drink lake water!"

"It seems like a different world altogether," said Migwan, looking out across the miles of factory-covered "flats." She was perfectly fascinated by the rolling mills, with their rows of black stacks standing out against the sky like organ pipes, and by the long trains of oil-tank cars curving through the valley like huge worms, the divisions giving the effect of body sections.

While the Winnebagos were gliding along among scenes strange and new, Hinpoha was vainly trying to comfort herself for having to stay at home by catching in a bottle the bees which were crawling in and out of the cosmos blossoms in the garden. Interesting as the bees were, however, they could not keep her thoughts from turning to the Winnebagos afloat on the river, and it was a very doleful face that bent over the flowers. Her dismal reflections were interrupted by the sharp voice of Aunt Phoebe calling her to come in. "What is it?" she asked listlessly, as she came up on the porch.

"Mrs. Evans is here," said her aunt in the doorway, "and she has asked to see you." Hinpoha was very glad to see Mrs. Evans, who rose smilingly and took her hands in hers.

"How thin you are getting, child!" she exclaimed, smoothing back the red curls. "I don't believe you get out enough. By the way," she said to Aunt Phoebe, "may I borrow this girl for to-day? I have considerable driving about to do and it is rather tiresome going alone. Gladys has gone on an all-day boat ride."

Aunt Phoebe could not very well refuse, for driving about in a machine with an older woman was a very proper form of recreation indeed, in her estimation.

Hinpoha flew upstairs and deposited her bottle of bees on the table in her room for future observation and started off with Mrs. Evans. "We will not be back for lunch, and possibly not for supper," said Gladys's mother as she bade Aunt Phoebe a gracious good-bye, "but it will not be long after that."

"And now for a grand spin," she said, as she started the car and sent it crackling through the dry leaves on the pavement.

"Now I see why the Indians named this river 'Cuyahoga,' or 'Crooked,'" said Migwan, as they rounded bend after bend in the stream. "It coils back on itself like a snake, and I have already counted seven coils within the city limits. I didn't believe it when the captain of a freighter told me that there was a place in the river which his boat couldn't pass because two sharp turns came so near together, but now I see how that could easily be possible."

As the launch putt-putt-putt-ed steadily up the river the water gradually became less black, and the factories along the shore gave way to open stretches of country. By noon they reached the dam and went ashore to look for a place to build a fire. They were in a deep gorge, its steep sides thickly covered with flaming maples and oaks, and brilliant sumachs, stretching on either side as far as they could reach. "It's too gorgeous to seem real," said Nyoda, shading her eyes and looking down the valley; "where does Mother Nature keep her pot of 'Diamond Dyes' in the summer time?"

High up along the top of one of the cliffs a narrow road wound along, and as Nyoda stood looking into the distance she saw an automobile coming along this road. When it was directly above her it stopped and two people got out, a woman and a girl. The sunlight fell on a mass of red curls on the girl's head. "Hinpoha!" exclaimed Nyoda in amazement. From above came floating down a far-echoing yodel—the familiar Winnebago call. The girls all looked up in surprise to see Hinpoha scrambling down the face of the cliff, and aiding Mrs. Evans to descend.

"Why, mother!" called Gladys, running up to meet her.

The surprise at the meeting was mutual. Mrs. Evans, spinning along the country roads, had no idea she was hard on the trail of her daughter and the other Winnebagos until she came suddenly upon them after they had gotten out of the launch. "Can't you stay and spend the day with us, now that you're here?" they pleaded.

Hinpoha's longing soul looked out of her eyes, but she answered, "I'm afraid not. Aunt Phoebe wouldn't approve."

"Did she say you couldn't?" asked Sahwah.

"No," said Hinpoha, "for I never even asked her if I might go along with you in the launch. I knew it would be no use."

"Oh, please stay," tempted some of the girls; "your aunt'll never know the difference."

"Oh, I couldn't do that," said Hinpoha in a tone of horror. A little approving smile crept around the corners of Nyoda's eyes as she heard Hinpoha so resolutely bidding Satan get behind her. Mrs. Evans was genuinely sorry they had encountered the girls, because it made it so much harder for Hinpoha.

"I wonder," she said musingly, "if I drove on to a house in the road and telephoned your aunt that she would let you stay?"

"You might try," said Hinpoha doubtfully. Mrs. Evans thought it was worth trying. She found a house with a telephone and got Aunt Phoebe on the wire. With the utmost tact she explained how they had met the girls accidently, and that she had taken a notion that she would like to spend the day with them, but of course she could not do so unless Hinpoha would be allowed to stay with her, as she had charge of her for the day. What was Aunt Phoebe to do? She was not equal to telling the admired Mrs. Evans to forego her pleasure because of Hinpoha, and gave a grudging consent to her keeping her niece with her on the condition that she would bring her home in the machine and not let her come back in the launch with the Winnebagos. Jubilant, they returned to the girls in the gorge and told the good news.

"Cheer for Mrs. Evans," cried Sahwah, and the Winnebagos gave it with a hearty good will.

Hinpoha, with Sahwah close beside her, began I searching for firewood industriously. "It seems just like last summer," she said, chopping sticks with Sahwah's hatchet. The two had wandered off a short distance from the others, following a tiny footpath. Suddenly they came upon a huge rock formation, that looked like an immense fireplace, about forty feet wide and twenty or more feet high. Under that great stone arch a dozen spits, each big enough to hold a whole ox, might easily have swung. Sahwah and Hinpoha looked at it in amazement and then called for the other girls to come and see.

"Why, that's the 'Old Maid's Kitchen,'" said Mrs. Evans, when she arrived on the scene. "I've been here before. Just why it should be called the Old Maid's Kitchen is more than I can tell, for it looks like the fireplace belonging to the grand-mother of all giantesses."

"Let's build our fire inside of it," said Nyoda.

"The original 'Old Maid' had a convenience that didn't usually go with open fireplaces," said Gladys, "and that is running water," and she held her cup under a tiny stream that trickled out between two rocks, cold as ice and clear as crystal.

"Wouldn't this be a grand place for a Ceremonial Meeting?" said Migwan, as they all stood round the blazing fire roasting "wieners" and bacon. The Kitchen had a floor of smooth slabs of rock, and the arch of the fireplace formed a roof over their heads, while its wide opening afforded them a wonderful view of the gorge.

"Whenever you want to come here again, just say so," said Mrs. Evans, "and I'll bring you down in the machine." Mrs. Evans was enjoying herself as much as any of the girls. It was the first time she had ever cooked wieners and bacon over an open fire on green sticks, and she was perfectly delighted with the experience. "If my husband could only see me now," she said, laughing like a girl as she dropped her last wiener in the dirt and calmly washed it off in the trickling stream. "How good this hot cocoa tastes!" she exclaimed, drinking down a whole cupful without stopping. "What kind is it?"

"Camp Fire Girl Cocoa," answered the girls.

"What kind is that?" asked Mrs. Evans.

"It is a brand that is put up by a New York firm for the Camp Fire Girls to sell," answered Nyoda.

"Why have we never had any of this at our house?" asked Mrs. Evans, turning to Gladys.

"You have always insisted that you would use no other kind than Van Horn's," replied Gladys, "so I thought there would be no use in mentioning it."

"I like this better than Van Horn's," said her mother. "Is there any to be had now?"

"There certainly is," answered Nyoda. "We are trying to dispose of a hundred-can lot to pay our annual dues."

"Let me have a dozen cans," said Mrs. Evans. "I will serve Camp Fire

Girl Cocoa to my Civic Club next Wednesday afternoon. I——"

Here a terrific shriek from Migwan brought them all to their feet. She had been poking about in the corner of the Kitchen, when something had suddenly jumped out at her, unfolded itself like a fan and was whirling around her head. "It's a bat!" cried Sahwah, and they all laughed heartily at Migwan's fright. The bat wheeled around, blind in the daylight, and went bumping against the girls, causing them to run in alarm lest it should get entangled in their hair. It finally found its way back to the dark corner of the Kitchen and hung itself up neatly the way Migwan had found it and the dinner proceeded.

"What kind of a bat was it?" asked Gladys.

"Must have been a bacon bat," said Sahwah, dodging the acorn that

Hinpoha threw at her for making a pun.

"Tell us a new game to play, Nyoda," said Gladys, "or Sahwah will go right on making puns."

"Here is one I thought of on the way down," answered Nyoda. "Think of all the things that you know are manufactured in Cleveland, or form an important part of the shipping industry. Then we'll go around the circle, naming them in alphabetical order. Each girl may have ten seconds in which to think when her turn comes, and if she misses she is out of the game. She may only come in again by supplying a word when another has missed, before the next girl in the circle can think of one."

"And let the two that hold out the longest have the first ride in the canoe," suggested Sahwah.

The game started. Nyoda had the first chance. "Automobiles," she began.

"Bricks," said Gladys.

"Clothing," said Migwan.

"Drugs," said Sahwah.

"Engines," said Hinpoha.

"Flour," said Mrs. Evans.

"Gasoline," said Nakwisi.

"Hardware," said Chapa.

"Iron," said Medmangi.

Nyoda hesitated, fishing for a "J." "One, two, three, four, five, six," began Sahwah.

"Jewelry!" cried Nyoda on the tenth count.

"Knitted goods," continued Gladys.

"Lamps," said Migwan.

"Macaroni," said Sahwah.

"That reminds me," said Mrs. Evans, "I meant to order some macaroni to-day and forgot it."

"N," said Hinpoha, "N,—why, Nothing!" The girls laughed at the witty application, but she was ruled out nevertheless.

"Nails," said Mrs. Evans.

"Oil," said Nakwisi.

"Paint," said Chapa.

Medmangi sat down. Nyoda began to count. "Quadrupeds!" cried Medmangi hastily.

"Explain yourself," said Nyoda.

"Tables and chairs," said Medmangi. The girls shouted in derision, but

Nyoda ruled the answer in, and the game proceeded.

"Refrigerators," said Nyoda.

"Salt," said Gladys.

"Tents," said Migwan, with a reminiscent sigh.

"Umbrellas," said Sahwah.

Mrs. Evans fell down on "V." "Varnish," said Chapa.

"W" was too much for Medmangi. "Wire," said Nyoda.

"X," said Sahwah, "there is no such thing. Oh, yes, there is, too;

Xylophones, they're made here."

Gladys and Migwan met their Waterloo on "Y." "Yeast," said Nyoda.

"Z," sent Chapa and Nakwisi to the dummy corner and it came back to

Sahwah. "Zerolene," she said.

"What's that?" they all cried.

"I don't know," she answered, "but I saw it on one of the big oil tanks as we passed."

Sahwah and Nyoda won the right to take the first paddle in the Keewaydin. They carried the canoe on their heads, portage fashion, around the dam, and launched it up above, where the confined waters had spread out into a wide pond. "Oh, what a joy to dip a paddle again!" sighed Sahwah blissfully, sending the Keewaydin flying through the water with long, vigorous strokes. "I'd love to paddle all the way home." She had completely forgotten that there was such a thing as school and lessons in the world. She was the Daughter of the River, and this was a joyous homecoming.

"Time to go back and let the rest have a turn," said Nyoda. Reluctantly Sahwah steered the canoe around and returned to the waiting group. Mrs. Evans watched with interest as Gladys and Hinpoha pushed out from shore. Could this be her once frail daughter, who had despised all strenuous sports and hated water above all things, who was swinging her paddle so lustily and steering the Keewaydin so skilfully? What was this strange Something that the Camp Fire had instilled into her? She caught her breath with the beauty of it, as the girls glided along between the radiant banks, the two paddles flashing in and out in perfect rhythm. They were singing a favorite boating song, and their voices floated back on the breeze:

"Through the mystic haze of the autumn days

Like a phantom ghost I glide,

Where the big moose sees the crimson trees

Mirrored on the silver tide,

And the blood red sun when day is done

Sinks below the hill,

The night hawk swoops, the lily droops,

And all the world is still!"

Sahwah lingered on the river after the others had gone in a body to try to climb to the top of the rocky fireplace. She was all alone in the Keewaydin, and sent it darting around like a water spider on the surface of the stream. So absorbed was she in the joy of paddling that she did not see a sign on a tree beside the river which warned people in boats to go no further than that point, neither did she realize the significance of the quicker progress which the Keewaydin was making. When she did realize that she was getting dangerously near the edge of the dam, and attempted to turn back, she discovered to her horror that it was impossible to turn back. The Keewaydin was being swept helplessly and irresistibly onward. Recent rains had swollen the stream and the water was pouring over the dam. Sahwah screamed aloud when she saw the peril in which she was. Nyoda and Mrs. Evans and the girls, standing up on the rocks, turned and saw her. Help was out of the question. Frozen to the spot they saw her rushing along to that descent of waters. Gladys moaned and covered her face with her hands. Below the falls the great rocks jutted out, jagged and bare. Any boat going over would be dashed to pieces.

The Keewaydin shot forward, gaining speed with every second. The roar of the falls filled Sahwah's ears. Not ten feet from the brink a rock jutted up a little above the surface, just enough to divide the current into two streams. When the Keewaydin reached this point it turned sharply and was hurled into the current nearest the shore. On the bank right at the brink of the falls stood a great willow tree, its long branches drooping far out over the water. It was one chance in a million and Sahwah saw it. As she passed under the tree she reached up and caught hold of a branch, seized it firmly and jumped clear of the canoe, which went over the falls almost under her feet. Then, swinging along by her arms, she reached the shore and stood in safety. It had all happened so quickly the girls could hardly comprehend it. Gladys, who had hidden her eyes to shut out the dreadful sight, heard an incredulous shout from the girls and looked down to see the Keewaydin landing on the rocks below, empty, and Sahwah standing on the bank.

"How did you ever manage to do it?" gasped Hinpoha, when they had surrounded her with exclamations of joy and amazement. "You're a heroine again."

"You're nothing of the sort," said Nyoda. "It was sheer foolhardiness or carelessness that got you into that scrape. A girl who doesn't know enough to keep out of the current isn't to be trusted with a canoe, no matter what a fine paddler she is. I certainly thought better of you than that, Sahwah. I never used to have the slightest anxiety when you were on the water, I had such a perfect trust in your common sense, but now I can never feel quite sure of you again."

Sahwah hung her head in shame, for she felt the truth of Nyoda's words. "I think you can trust me after this," she said humbly. "I have learned my lesson." She was not likely to forget the horror of the moment when she had heard the water roaring over the dam and thought her time had come. Sahwah liked to be thought clever as well as daring, and it was certainly far from clever to run blindly into danger as she had done. She sank dejectedly down on the bank, feeling disgraced forever in the eyes of the Winnebagos.

"Girls," said Mrs. Evans, wishing to take their minds off the fright they had received, "do you know that we are not many miles from one of the model dairy farms of the world? I could take you over in the car and bring you back here in time to go home in the launch."

"Let's do it, Nyoda," begged all the Winnebagos, and into the machine they piled. When they were still far in the distance they could see the high towers of the barns rising in the air. "We're nearly there," said Mrs. Evans; "here is the beginning to the cement fence that runs all the way around the four-thousand-acre farm." Mrs. Evans knew some of the people in charge of the farm and they had no difficulty gaining admittance. That visit to the Carter Farm was a long-remembered one. The girls walked through the long stables exclaiming at everything they saw.

"Why, there's an electric fan in each stall!" gasped Migwan, "and the windows are screened!"

"Oo, look at the darling calf," gurgled Hinpoha, on her knees before one of the stalls, caressing a ten-thousand-dollar baby.

"It doesn't look a bit like its mother," observed Nyoda, comparing it with the cow standing beside it.

"That isn't its mother, that's its nurse," said the man who was showing them around.

"Its what?" said Nyoda. Then the man explained that the milk from the blooded cows was too valuable to be fed to calves, as it commanded a high price on the market, and so a herd of common cows were kept to feed the aristocratic babies. The lovely little creatures were as tame as kittens and allowed the girls to fondle them to their hearts' content. Sometimes a pair of polished horns would come poking between a calf and the visitors, and a soft-eyed cow would view the proceedings with a comically anxious face, and then it was easy to tell which calf was with its mother.

In one of the largest stalls they saw the champion Guernsey of the world. Her coat was like satin and her horns were polished until they shone. She did not seem to be in the least set up on account of her great reputation and thrust out her nose in the friendliest manner possible to be patted and fussed over. She eyed Gladys, who stood next to her, with amiable curiosity, and then suddenly licked her face. Mrs. Evans watched Gladys in surprise. Instead of quivering all over with disgust as she would have a year ago she simply laughed and patted the cow's nose. "What is going to happen?" said Mrs. Evans to herself, "Gladys isn't afraid of cows any more!" But the most interesting part came when the cows were milked. They were driven into another barn for this performance and their heads fastened into sort of metal hoops suspended from the ceiling. These turned in either direction and caused them no discomfort, but kept them standing in one place. The milking was done with vacuum-suction machines run by electricity and took only a short time.

When the girls had watched the process as long as they wished they were taken to see the prize hogs and chickens, and then went through the hot houses. There were rows and rows of glass houses filled with grapes, the great bunches hanging down from the roof and threatening to fall with their own weight. And one did fall, just as they were going through, and came smashing down in the path at their feet. Nakwisi ran to pick it up and the guide said she might have it, adding that such a bunch, unbruised, sold for twenty-five cents in the city market. "Oh, how delicious!" cried Nakwisi,' tasting the grapes and dividing them among the girls. Mrs. Evans bought a basketful and let them eat all they wanted. In some of the hothouses tangerines were growing, and in some persimmons, while others were given over to the raising of roses, carnations and rare orchids. It was a trip through fairyland for the girls, and they could hardly tear themselves away when the time came.

"There is something else I must show you while we are in the neighborhood," said Mrs. Evans, as they passed through Akron. "Does anybody know what two historical things are near here?" Nobody knew. Mrs. Evans began humming, "John Brown's Body Lies A-mouldering in the Grave."

"What has that to do with it?" asked Gladys.

"Everything, with one of them," said Mrs. Evans.

"Did you know that John Brown, owner of the said body, was born in

Akron, and there is a monument here to his memory?"

"Oh how lovely," cried Migwan, "let us see it." So Mrs. Evans drove them over to the monument and they all stood around it and sang "John Brown's Body" in his honor.

"Now, what's the other thing?" they asked.

"I believe I know," said Nyoda. "Doesn't the old Portage Trail run through here somewhere?"

"That's it," said Mrs. Evans.

Then Nyoda told them about the Portage Path of Indian days, before the canal was built, that extended from Lake Erie to the Ohio River. "The part that runs through Akron is still called Portage Path," said Mrs. Evans, and the girls were eager to see it.

"Why, it's nothing but a paved street!" exclaimed Migwan in disappointment, when they had reached the historical spot.

"That's all it is now," answered Mrs. Evans, "but it is built over the old Portage Trail, and some of these old trees undoubtedly shaded the original path." In the minds of the girls the handsome residences faded from sight, and in place of the wide street they saw the narrow path trailing off through the forest, with dusky forms stealing along it on their long journey southward.

"It's time to strike our own trail now," said Nyoda, breaking the silence, and they started back to the river. Every one was anxious to make it as pleasant as possible for Hinpoha, and the jests came thick and fast as they drove along. "Who is the best Latin scholar here?" asked Nyoda.

"I am," said Sahwah, mischievously.

"Then you can undoubtedly tell me what Caesar said on the Fourth of

July, 45 B.C." said Nyoda.

"I don't seem to recollect," said Sahwah.

"Then read for yourself," said Nyoda, scribbling a few words on a leaf from her notebook and handing it to her.

"What's this?" said Sahwah, spelling out the words. On the paper was written,

Quis crudis enim rufus, albus et expiravit.

Sahwah tried to translate. "Quis, who; crudis, raw; enim—what's enim?"

"For," answered Migwan.

"And expiravit" said Sahwah, "what's that from?"

"Expiro" answered Migwan, "expirare, expiravi, expiratus. It means 'blow,' 'Expiravit' is 'have blown.'"

"Rufus is 'red,'" continued Sahwah, "and is albus 'white'?" Migwan nodded, and Sahwah went back to the beginning and began to read: "Who raw for red white and have blown."

Nyoda shouted. "That last word is blew, not have blown" she said.

"I have it!" cried Migwan, jumping up. "It's 'Who raw for the red, white and blew.' 'Hoorah for the red, white and blue!'"

"Such wit!" said Sahwah, laughing with the rest.

"Now, I'll make a motto for Sahwah," said Migwan, seizing the pencil. Migwan was a Senior and took French, and having a sudden inspiration, she wrote, "Pas de lieu Rhone que nous!" The girls could not translate it and Nyoda puzzled over it for a long time.

"I don't seem to be able to make anything out of it," she said at length.

"Don't try to translate it," said Migwan, "just read it out loud," Nyoda complied and Sahwah caught it immediately.

"It's 'Paddle your own canoe!" she cried.

Thus, laughing and joking, they followed the road back to the dam and embarked in the launch with all speed, for the sun was already sinking beneath the treetops and they had a two-hour ride ahead of them. Mrs. Evans took Hinpoha back in the machine and delivered her to her aunt safe and sound at eight o'clock, with many expressions of pleasure at the fun she had had with the Camp Fire Girls, which were intended as seeds to be planted in Aunt Phoebe's mind.

"I think your mother's a perfect dear," said Sahwah to Gladys on the trip home. "I used to be frightened to death of her, because she always looked so straight-laced and proper, but she isn't like that at all. She's a regular Camp Fire Girl!"

CHAPTER V.

A COASTING PARTY.

The memory of that happy day sustained Hinpoha through many of the trials that came to her in the days that followed. It seemed that everything she did brought down the wrath of her aunt in some way or another. For instance, she left a bottle of bees standing on the table in her room, and Aunt Phoebe's dog Silky, who had been in the habit of going into the room and chewing Hinpoha's painted paddle, knocked the bottle over and let the bees out, getting badly stung in the process. Then there was a scene with Aunt Phoebe because she had brought the bees in. This and a dozen more incidents of a similar nature made Hinpoha despair of ever gaining the good will of her aunt. Thus the autumn wore away to winter and as yet the Desert of Waiting had borne nothing but thorns.

Gladys's progress through school was like the advance of a conquering hero. Although she had just entered this fall she was already one of the most popular girls in school. She had that fair, delicate prettiness which invariably appeals to boys, and an open, unaffected manner which endeared her to the girls. Beside her very lovable personality she had a background which was almost certain to insure popularity to a girl. She was rich and lived in a great house on a fashionable avenue; she had a little electric car all her own, and she wore the smartest clothes of any girl in school. Her fame as a dancer soon spread and she was in constant demand at school entertainments. Nyoda watched her a trifle anxiously at first. She was just a little afraid that Gladys's head would be turned with all the homage paid her, or that, blinded by her present success, she would lose the deeper meanings of life and be nothing but a butterfly after all. But she need not have feared. Gladys's experience in camp had kindled a fire in her that would never be extinguished as long as life guarded the flame. Having changed her Camp Fire name from Butterfly to Real Woman, she was anxious to prove her right to the name. So she worked diligently to win new honors which made her efficient in the home as well as those which helped her to shine in society.

Mrs. Evans was returning from an afternoon card party. She was tired and her head ached and she felt out of sorts. A remark which she had overheard during the afternoon stayed in her mind and made her cross. Two ladies on the other side of a large screen near which she was sitting were discussing a campaign in which they were interested to raise funds for a certain philanthropy. "I am going to ask Mrs. Evans if she would not like to subscribe one hundred dollars," said the one lady.

"So much?" asked the other in an uncertain voice, "I don't believe I would if I were you."

"Why not?" asked the first lady.

"Haven't you heard," replied the second lady, with the air of imparting a delicious secret, "that Mr. Evans is on the verge of financial ruin?"

"No," replied the second in a tone of lively interest, "I haven't. Who told you so?"

"A great many people are saying so," continued the first. "Do you know that they took their daughter out of the private school she had been attending and sent her to public school this year? They must be hard up if they can't pay school bills any more."

"It certainly looks like it," said the first lady.

"Possibly I had better not ask Mrs. Evans for any subscription at all. It might embarrass her, poor thing." The voices trailed off and Mrs. Evans was left feeling decidedly annoyed. She was the kind of woman who rarely discussed other people's affairs, and likewise disliked having her own discussed by other people. The thought that some folks might misconstrue Gladys's entering the public school to mean that her father was about to fail in business, first amused, and then irritated her. Nothing like that could be farther from correct, but the thought came to her that such rumors floating around might have some effect on Mr. Evans's standing in the business world. She began to wonder if after all it had not been a mistake to take Gladys out of Miss Russell's school in the middle of her course.

Thinking cynical thoughts about the gossiping abilities of most people, she drove up the long driveway and entered the house. The long hall with its wide staircase and large, splendidly furnished rooms opening on either side, struck her as being cold and gloomy. The polished chairs and tables shone dully in the fast waning light of the December afternoon, cheerless and unfriendly looking. The house suddenly seemed to her to be less a home than a collection of furniture. For the moment she almost hated the wealth which made it necessary to maintain this vast and magnificent display. The women she had played cards with that afternoon seemed shallow and artificial. Life was decidedly uninteresting just then. She went upstairs and took off her wraps and came down again, aimlessly. Gladys was nowhere in sight, which made the house seem lonelier than ever, for with Gladys around there would have been somebody to talk to. At the foot of the stairs she paused. She could hear some one singing in a distant part of the house. "Katy's happy, anyway," she said with a sigh, "if she feels like singing in that hot kitchen," A desire for company led her out to the kitchen. It was not Katy, however, who greeted her when she opened the door. It was Gladys—Gladys with a big apron on and her sleeves rolled up, just taking from the oven a pan of golden brown muffins. The room was filled with the delicious odor of freshly baked dough.

Gladys looked up with a smile when she saw her mother in the doorway. "How do you like the new cook?" she asked. "Katy went home sick this afternoon and I thought I would get supper myself." The kitchen looked so cheerful and inviting that Mrs. Evans came in and sat down. Gladys began mixing up potatoes for croquettes.

"Can't I do something?" asked her mother.

"Why, yes," said Gladys, bringing out another apron and tying it around her waist, "you heat the fat to fry these in." Mrs. Evans and Gladys had never had such a good time together. Gladys had planned the entire menu and her mother meekly followed her directions as to what to do next. She and Gladys frolicked around the kitchen with increasing hilarity as the supper progressed. Never before had there existed such a comradeship between them.

"Do you think this is seasoned right?" asked Mrs. Evans, holding out a spoonful of white sauce for Gladys to taste.

"A little more salt," said Gladys judicially. Mrs. Evans had forgotten her irritation of the afternoon. The conversation which had aroused her ire before now struck her as humorous.

"If Mrs. Davis and Mrs. Jones could only see me now," she thought with an inward chuckle, "doing my own cooking!" The half-formed plan of sending Gladys back to Miss Russell's the first of the year faded from her mind. Send Gladys away? Why, she was just beginning to enjoy her company! Another plan presented itself to her mind. In the Christmas vacation Gladys should give a party which would forever dispel any doubts about the soundness of their financial standing. Her brain was already at work on the details. Gladys should have a dress from Madame Charmant's in New York. They would have Waldstein, from the Symphony Orchestra, with a half dozen of his best players, furnish the music. There would be expensive prizes and favors for the games. Mrs. Davis and Mrs. Jones would have a chance to alter their opinions when their daughters brought home accounts of the affair. She planned the whole thing while she was eating her supper.

After supper Gladys washed the dishes and her mother wiped them, and they put them away together. Then Gladys began to get ready to go to Camp

Fire meeting and Mrs. Evans reluctantly prepared to go out for the evening. The nearer ready she was the more disinclined she felt to go. "Those Jamieson musicales are always such a bore," she said to herself wearily. "They never have good singers—my Gladys could do better than any of them—and they are interminable. Father looks tired to death, and I know he would rather stay at home. Gladys," she called, looking into her daughter's room, "where is your Camp Fire meeting to-night?"

"At the Brewsters'," answered Gladys.

"Do you ever have visitors?" continued her mother.

"Why, yes," answered Gladys, "we often do."

"Do you mind if you have one to-night?" asked Mrs. Evans.

"Certainly not," replied Gladys.

"Well, then, I'm coming along," said her mother.

"Will you?" cried Gladys. "Oh goody!" The Winnebagos were surprised and delighted when Mrs. Evans appeared with Gladys. Since that Saturday's outing she had held a very warm place in their affections.

"Come in, mother," called Sahwah; "you might as well join the group too, we have one guest. This is Mrs. Evans, Gladys's mother," she said, when her mother appeared after hastily brushing back her hair and putting on a white apron. The two women held out their hands in formal greeting, and then changed their minds and fell on each other's necks.

"Why, Molly Richards!" exclaimed Mrs. Evans.

"Why, Helen Adamson!" gasped Mrs. Brewster. The Winnebagos looked on, mystified.

"You can't introduce me to your mother," said Mrs. Evans to Sahwah, laughing at her look of surprise. "We were good friends when we were younger than you. Do you remember the time," she said, turning back to Mrs. Brewster, "when you drew a picture of Miss Scully in your history and she found it and made you stand up in front of the room and hold it up so the whole class could see it?"

"Do you remember the time," returned Mrs. Brewster, "when we ran away from school to see the Lilliputian bazaar and your mother was there and walked you out by the ear?" Thus the flow of reminiscences went on.

"How little I thought," said Mrs. Evans, "when I first saw Sarah Ann going around with Gladys, that she was your daughter!"

"How little I thought," said Mrs. Brewster, "when Gladys began coming here, that she was your daughter!"

"How many more of these girls' mothers are our old schoolmates, I wonder?" said Mrs. Evans.

"Let's meet them and find out," said Mrs. Brewster. "Here, you girls," she said, "every one of you go home and get your mother." Delightedly the girls obeyed, and the mothers came, a little backward, some of them, a little shy, pathetically eager, and decidedly breathless. Migwan's mother, Mrs. Gardiner, had known Mrs. Brewster in her girlhood, and Nakwisi's mother had known Mrs. Evans, and Chapa's and Medmangi's mothers had known each other. What a happy reunion that was, and what a chorus of "Don't you remembers" rose on every side! Tears mingled with the laughter when they spoke of the death of Mrs. Bradford, whom most of them had known in their school days.

"Do you remember," said one of the mothers, "how we used to go coasting down the reservoir hill? You girls have never seen the old reservoir. It was levelled off years ago."

"I'd enjoy going coasting yet," said Mrs. Brewster.

"Let's!" said Mrs. Evans. "The snow is just right."

Girls and mothers hurried into their coats and out into the frosty air. The street sloped down sharply, and the middle of the road was filled with flying bobsleds, as the young people of the neighborhood took advantage of the snowy crust. Sahwah brought out her brother's bob, which he was not using this evening, and piled the whole company on behind her. She could steer as well as a boy. Down the long street they shot, from one patch of light into another as they passed the lamp posts. The mothers shrieked with excitement and held on for dear life. "Oh," panted Mrs. Brewster when they came to a standstill at the bottom of the slope, "is there anything in the world half so exciting and delightful as coasting?" Down they went, again and again, laughing all the way, and causing many another bobload to look around and wonder who the jolly ladies were. Most of the mothers lost their breath in the swift rush and had to be helped up the hill to the starting point. Once Sahwah turned too short at the bottom of the street and upset the whole sledful into a deep pile of snow, from which they emerged looking like snowmen. "Oh-h-h," sputtered Mrs. Brewster, "the snow is all going down inside of my collar! Sarah Ann, you wretch, you deserve to have your face washed for that!" She picked up a great lump of snow and hurled it deftly at Sahwah's head. It struck its mark and flew all to pieces, much of it going down the back of her neck.

"This coasting is all right," said Mrs. Gardiner, "but, oh, that walk up hill!"

Mrs. Evans spied her machine standing in front of the Brewster house, and it gave her an idea. "Why not tie the bob to the machine," she said, "and go for a regular ride?" This suggestion was hailed with great joy, and carried out with alacrity.

"Would you like to drive, mother?" asked Gladys.

"No, indeed!" said her mother. "I'm out sleigh-riding to-night. You get in and drive it yourself!" Gladys complied, with Migwan up beside her for company, and away they flew up one street and down another and through the park. And just as they were going around a curve, Sahwah, who sat at the front end of the sled, untied the rope, and away went the machine around the corner, and left them stranded in the snow. Gladys felt the release of the trailer, but pretended that she knew nothing about it, and drove ahead at full speed, and traveling in a circle, came up behind the marooned voyagers and surprised them with a hearty laugh. This time she towed them back to Sahwah's house, where they drank hot cocoa to warm themselves up, and all declared they had never had such fun in their lives.

"And to think how near I came to missing this!" said Mrs. Evans, as she and Gladys were driving home, and she shivered when she remembered how she had almost gone to the musicale.

CHAPTER VI.

GLADYS UPHOLDS THE FAMILY CREDIT.

Mrs. Evans confided her plans for a Christmas week party to Gladys the day following the snow frolic, and Gladys was delighted with the idea. She dearly loved to entertain her friends. The frock was ordered from New York and Mrs. Evans and Gladys spent long hours working out the details of the affair. Rumors of the party and the dress Gladys was to have leaked out to the Winnebagos and from them to the whole class. Every one was on tiptoe to find out who would be invited. Mrs. Davis and Mrs. Jones, hearing the talk about the coming function, began to wonder if they were on the right track after all in regard to the Evans fortune. Two weeks before Christmas the invitations came out. Twenty-five girls and twenty-five boys, mostly from the high school class, were asked. What a flutter of satisfaction there was among those who had been invited, and what a disappointment among those who had not been, and what consultations about dresses among the favored ones!

This question was an acute one with Migwan. She had not had a new party dress for several years, and in the present state of their finances she could not get one now. She looked at the old one, faded and spotted, and shook her head despairingly. "I foresee where Miss Migwan develops a sudden illness on the night of the party," she said with tight lips, "unless I hear from my story in time." As if in answer to her thoughts the story came back the very next day. There was no letter from the editor concerning the merits or faults of the piece, only a printed rejection slip, but that stated that only typewritten manuscripts would be considered. Migwan's air castle tumbled about her ears. She had no typewriter and knew no one who had. Her experience did not include a knowledge of public stenographers, and even if she had thought of that way out the expense would have prevented her from having her story copied. Her dream of fame and wealth was short-lived, and the world was stale, flat and unprofitable. The house was not yet rented, as the repairs had been delayed again and again. It would be another month at least before that would be a paying proposition. Hearing the other girls talk about Gladys's party all the time filled her with desperation. She began to shun the Winnebagos. The keen zest went out of her studying and even her beloved Latin lost its savor.

Nyoda finally noticed it. Migwan failed to recite in English class for two days in succession, which was an unheard-of thing. Nyoda thought that Migwan had her head so full of the coming party that she was neglecting her lessons, and said so, half banteringly, as Migwan lingered after class to pick up some papers she had dropped on the floor. That was the last straw, and Migwan burst into tears. Nyoda was all sympathy in a moment. Now Nyoda happened to have the "seeing eye," with which some people are blessed, and had surmised, from certain little signs she had observed, that Migwan had written something or other, and sent it away to a magazine. She knew only too well what the outcome would be, and her heart ached when she thought of Migwan's coming disappointment. Therefore, when Migwan, quickly recovering her composure, said calmly, "It's nothing, Nyoda; I simply tried to do something and failed," Nyoda asked quietly, "Did your story come back?"

Migwan looked at her in amazement. "How did you know I had written any story?" she asked.

"Oh, a little bird told me," replied Nyoda lightly. "Cheer up. All the famous authors had their first work rejected. You have achieved the first mark of fame." Migwan smiled wanly. Her tragedies always seemed to lose their sting in the light of Nyoda's optimism. She told her about the necessity for a typewriter. "I could have told you that to begin with, if you had asked my humble advice," replied Nyoda. "But if a miserable writing machine is all that stands between you and fame and fortune, your fortune is already made. The woman whose rooms I am living in has one in her possession. It belongs to her son, I believe, but as he is at present in China there is no danger of his wanting it for some time. She has offered to let me use it on several occasions, and I don't doubt but what we can make some arrangement to accommodate you."

The world seemed a pretty good place of habitation after all to Migwan that day when she went home from school, in spite of the fact that she had no dress to wear to the party. The situation began to appear faintly humorous to her. Here was all the interest centered on what Gladys was going to wear, when all the time the real, vital question was what she was going to wear! What a commotion there would be if the other Winnebagos knew the truth! Her thoughts began to beat themselves, into rhythm as she walked home through the crunching snow:

"Broke, broke, broke,

And such clothes in the windows I see!

And I would that my purse could answer

The demands that are made on she!

"O well for the millionaire's wife,

Who can pay eighty bones for a shawl,

And well for the African maids,

Who don't need any clothes at all!

"And the pennies, they all go

To the grocer, and so do the dimes,

But, O, for the little crepe meteor dress

I saw down in Oppenheim's!

"Broke, broke, broke,

And such styles in the windows I see!

What would I not give for the rest of the month

For the salary of John D!"

"Would you just as soon run up to the attic and get the blanket sheets out of the trunk?" asked her mother when she had finished her dinner. "I was cold in bed last night." Migwan went up promptly. She found the sheets and laid them out, and was then seized with a desire to rummage among the things in the trunk. She pawed over old valentines, bonnets of a by-gone day, lace mitts, and all the useless relics that are usually found in mother's trunk that had been her mother's. Down at the bottom, however, there was a paper package of considerable size. Migwan opened it carefully and brought to view a dress made of white brocaded satin, yellowed with age. A sudden inspiration struck her, and, laying it carefully on top of the blankets, she ran downstairs to her mother. "What is this dress?" she asked eagerly.

Mrs. Gardiner's face lighted tenderly when she saw it. "Why, that's my wedding dress," she said.

"Oh," said Migwan in a disappointed tone, laying the dress down.

"What did you want with it?" asked her mother.

"Why, I thought if it was just a dress," replied Migwan, "I could make it over to wear to Gladys's party, but of course if it is your wedding dress you wouldn't care to have it changed."

"I don't see why not," said Mrs. Gardiner. "It's no good as it is. I've never had it on since my wedding day. The material in that dress cost two dollars a yard and is better than what you get at that price nowadays." A sudden recollection illumined her face. "The night of the party is my wedding anniversary," she said. "There couldn't be a better occasion to wear it!"

"Would you really be willing to have me cut it up?" asked Migwan rapturously clasping her hands. That afternoon her head really was so full of party plans that she forgot to get her lessons. The dress was laid out on the dining room table and examined as to its possibilities. "I don't know but what it would be best to dye it some pretty shade of green or blue," said Mrs. Gardiner, after thinking the matter over. "It is too yellow to use as it is, and there is no time to bleach it properly." So it was ripped up and dyed Nile green, a shade which was particularly becoming to Migwan. There was enough goods in the train to make the entire dress, so there was no need to do any piecing.

Instead of avoiding the subject of the party, Migwan now joined happily in the discussions, and asked questions right and left about the best style in which to make her dress. She said nothing about the former function of that particular piece of goods. "Extravagant Migwan!" said Sahwah, "getting a satin dress for the party. My mother made me get silk poplin," Gladys's dress had arrived from New York, but she would not breathe a word in regard to it and the girls were wild with curiosity. Only Hinpoha was allowed to behold its glories, as a consolation for not being able to come to the party. Of course Hinpoha had been sworn to secrecy regarding it, but that did not keep her from rhapsodizing about it on general principles and pitching the girls' curiosity still higher.

Now there was one girl who had been invited to the party who said very little about it. This was Emily Meeks, who sat beside Gladys in the session room. Emily had also entered the class this fall, but, unlike Gladys, her path had not been marked by triumphs. She was timid and retiring, and after being three months in the class was little better known than she had been at first. The truth was that Emily was an orphan, working her way through High School by taking care of the children of one of the professors after school hours, and had neither money nor time to spend in the company of her classmates. Gladys was sorry for her because she always looked so sad and lonely, and, thinking to give her one good time at least to treasure up in the memory of her school days, invited her to the party. Emily accepted the invitation gratefully.

The night of the party came at last. Migwan's dress was finished and when she was finally arrayed in it she could compare favorably with the wealthiest girl in the crowd. She even wore her mother's high-heeled white satin wedding slippers with the little gold buckles, which fitted her perfectly. She skipped away happily with a good-bye kiss to her mother, who was tired out with her labors.

Gladys had relented at the last minute, and promised the Winnebagos that if they would come a half hour early they might help her dress. That was because the Winnebagos were closer kin to her than the rest of the girls, and it would be a shame to have any one else see the dress first. So they all gathered in Gladys's room, where the dress lay on the bed. It was of light blue chiffon, exquisitely hand embroidered in dainty-colored butterflies. "Oh-h," they gasped, not daring to touch it.

"There goes the bell!" exclaimed Gladys, "and I'm not even dressed. It's some of the boys, I hear their voices," she said presently, after listening for the sounds from below. "Run down, will you, girls, and entertain them until I come?"

The Winnebagos departed to act the part of hostesses for their friend and Gladys got hurriedly into her dress. Before she was ready to go down she heard a large group of girls arriving, then another delegation of boys. The orchestra had begun playing. Gladys's foot tapped the floor in time to the music as she fastened up the dress. "Just wait until they see me dance the Butterfly Dance," she was thinking, with innocent pride. She clasped the butterflies on her shoulders in place and with a last survey of herself in the glass she set forth to greet her guests. When she reached the head of the stairs the bell rang again and she paused to see who it was. From the hall upstairs she could get a view of the entire reception room without being seen herself. The last comer was Emily Meeks, whom the maid was relieving of her wraps. She was all alone, apparently at a loss what to do in company, and—dressed in a white skirt and middy blouse! Gladys could see the coldly amused glances some of the girls were bestowing on her, and the indifference with which she was being treated by the boys. Why did she come dressed in such a fashion? Gladys felt a little indignant at her. Then she reflected that Emily probably had nothing else to wear, and, besides, it didn't make any difference if one was dressed so plainly; there were enough brightly dressed girls to make the brilliant scene that she loved.

But at the same time a thought struck her which made her decidedly uncomfortable. It was, "How would you like to be the odd one in the crowd, and have all the others take notice of you because you didn't match your surroundings? To face a battery of eyes that were amused or scornful or pitying, according to the disposition of the owner of the eyes? To feel lonesome in the midst of a crowd and wish you were miles away?" With one foot on the top step Gladys hesitated. In her mind there rose a picture—the picture of her first night in camp when she had seen a Camp Fire

Ceremonial for the first time, when she felt lonesome and far away and out of place. Again she saw the figures circling around the fire and heard the words of their song:

"Whose hand above this blaze is lifted

Shall be with magic touch engifted

To warm the hearts of lonely mortals

Who stand without their open portals.

"Whoso shall stand

By this hearthstone

Flame fanned,

Shall never stand alone——"

And later the flame had been given into her keeping, and she was supposed to possess the magic touch to warm lonely hearts. She glanced at herself in the long mirror in the hall, and was struck afresh by the beauty of the dress. The shade of blue was just the right one to bring out the tint of her eyes and the gold of her hair. From head to foot she was a vision of loveliness such as delighted her dainty nature. One interpretation of "Seek Beauty" was to always dress as beautifully and becomingly as possible. Her mother was impatiently waiting for her to come down and show herself. Then she looked over the railing again. Emily Meeks had withdrawn from the groups of laughing girls and boys and had crept into a corner by herself. The words of the Fire Song echoed again in her ears:

"Whoso shall stand

By this hearthstone

Flame fanned,

Shall never stand alone!"

Gladys turned and fled to her room and resolutely began to unclasp the fasteners of her butterfly dress. A ripple of astonishment went through the rooms downstairs when she descended clad in a white linen skirt and a middy blouse. All the girls had heard about the dress from New York and were impatient to see it. Frances Jones and Caroline Davis stood right at the foot of the stairs waiting for Gladys to come down so they would not lose a detail of it, and Mrs. Evans was watching them to see what effect the butterfly dress would have on them. When Gladys came down dressed in a white skirt and middy she could not believe her eyes. She hurried forward and asked in a low voice what was the matter with the new dress.

"Nothing, mother," said Gladys sweetly, with such a beautiful smile that her mother dropped back in perplexity. Gladys advanced straight to Emily Meeks and greeted her first of all, with a friendly cordiality that put her at her ease at once. Emily, who had been dismayed when she found herself so conspicuous among all the brightly gowned girls, was reassured when she saw Gladys similarly clad, and never found out about that quick change of costume that had taken place after her coming. The other girls of course understood this fine little act of courtesy, and shamefacedly began to include Emily in their conversation and merrymaking.

So, if Mrs. Evans had counted on Gladys's dress that night to testify to the soundness of the Evans fortune she was destined to be disappointed; but on the other hand, if inborn courtesy is a sign of high birth and breeding, then Gladys had proven herself to be a princess of the royal blood.

CHAPTER VII.

HARD TIMES FOR POETS.

True to her word, Nyoda brought it about that Migwan might use the typewriter which belonged to her landlady, and every evening after her lessons were learned she worked diligently to master the keys. In a week or so she managed to copy her story and sent it out again. It came back as promptly as before, with the same kind of rejection slip. She sent it to another magazine and began writing a new one. She worked feverishly, and far beyond her strength. The room where the typewriter was was directly below Nyoda's sitting room, and hearing the machine still rattling after ten o'clock one night she calmly walked in and pulled Migwan away from the keys. Migwan protested. "It's past closing time," said Nyoda firmly.

"But I must finish this page," said Migwan.

"You must nothing of the kind," said Nyoda, forcing Migwan into her coat. "'Hold on to Health' does not mean work yourself to death. Hereafter you stop writing at nine o'clock or I will take the typewriter away from you."

"Oh, mayn't I stay until half past nine?" asked Migwan coaxingly.

"No, ma'm," said Nyoda emphatically. "Nine o'clock is the time. That's a bargain. As long as you keep your part of it you may use the typewriter, but as soon as you step over the line I go back on my part. Now remember, 'No checkee, no shirtee.'" And Migwan perforce had to submit.

The stories came back as fast as they were sent out, and Migwan began to have new sidelights on the charmed life supposedly led by authors and authoresses. The struggle to get along without getting into debt was becoming an acute one with the Gardiner family. Tom delivered papers during the week and helped out in a grocery store on Saturday, and his earnings helped slightly, but not much. Midwinter taxes on two houses ate up more than two weeks' income. With almost superhuman ingenuity Migwan apportioned their expenses so the money covered them. This she had to do practically alone, for her mother was as helpless before a column of figures as she would have been in a flood. Meat practically disappeared from the table. The big bag of nuts which Tom had gathered in the fall and which they had thought of only as a treat to pass around in the evening now became a prominent part of the menu. Dried peas and beans, boiled and made into soup, made their appearance on the table several times a week. Cornbread was another standby. Long years afterward Migwan would shudder at the sight of either bean soup or cornbread. She nearly wore out the cook book looking for new ways in which to serve potatoes, squash, turnips, onions and parsnips.

She soon discovered that most provisions could be bought a few cents cheaper in the market than in the stores, so every Saturday afternoon she made a trip downtown with a big market basket and bought the week's supply of butter, eggs and vegetables. At first the necessity for spending carfare cut into her profits, but she got around this in an adroit way that promised well for her future ability to handle her affairs to the best advantage. She tried a little publicity work to swing things around to suit her purpose. She simply exalted the joys of marketing until the other Winnebagos were crazy to do the family marketing, too. As soon as Gladys caught the fever her object was accomplished, for Gladys took all the girls to market in her father's big car and brought all their purchases home. So Migwan accomplished her own ends and gave the Winnebagos a new opportunity to pursue knowledge at the same time.

At Christmas time she had also fallen back on her ingenuity to produce the gifts she wished to give. There was no money at all to be spent for this purpose. Migwan took a careful stock of the resources of the house. The only promising thing she found was a leather skin which Hinpoha had given her the summer before for helping her write up the weekly Count in Hiawatha meter, which was outside of Hinpoha's range of talents. She considered the possibilities of that skin carefully. It must yield seven articles—a present for each of the Winnebagos. She decided on book covers. She wrote up seven different incidents of the summer camping trip in verse and copied them with the typewriter on rough yellow drawing paper, thinking to decorate each sheet. But Migwan had little artistic ability and soon saw that her decorations were not beautiful enough to adorn Christmas gifts. After spoiling several pages she gave up in disgust and threw the spoiled pages into the grate. The next morning she was cleaning out the grate and found the pieces of paper, only partially burned around the edges. She suddenly had an idea. The fire had burned a neat and artistic brown border around the writing. Why not burn all her sheets around the edges? Accordingly she set to work with a candle, and in a short time had her pages decorated in an odd and original way which could not fail to appeal to a Camp Fire Girl. Then she pasted the irregular pieces of yellow paper on straight pages of heavy brown paper, which brought out the burned edges beautifully. On the cover of each book she painted the symbol of the girl for whom it was intended, and on the inside of the back cover she painted her own. The Winnebagos were delighted with the books and took greater pride in showing them to their friends than they did their more expensive presents.

That piece of ingenuity was bread cast on the water for Migwan. Nyoda came to her one day while she was working her head off on the typewriter. "Could the authoress be persuaded to desist from her labors for a while?" she asked, tiptoeing around the room in a ridiculous effort to be quiet, which convulsed Migwan.

"Speak," said Migwan. "Your wish is already granted."

Nyoda sat down. "You remember that cunning little book you made me for Christmas?" she asked. Migwan nodded. "Well," continued Nyoda, "I was showing it to Professor Green the other night and he was quite carried away with it. He has a quantity of notes he took on a hunting trip last fall and wants to know if you will make them into a book like that for him. There will be quite a bit of work connected with it, as all the material will have to be copied on the typewriter and arranged in good order, and he is willing to pay two and a half dollars for your services. Would you be willing to do it?"

Would she be willing to do it? Would she see two and a half dollars lying in the street and not pick it up? The professor's notes were speedily secured and she set to work happily to transform them into an artistic record book. Her sister Betty grumbled a good deal these days because she was asked to do so much of the housework. Before Migwan took to typewriting at night Betty had been in the habit of staying out of the house until supper was ready, and then getting up from the table and going out again immediately, leaving Migwan to get supper and wash the dishes. It was easier to do the work herself than to argue with Betty about it, and if she appealed to her mother Mrs. Gardiner always said, "Just leave the dishes and I'll do them alone," so rather than have her mother do them Migwan generally washed and wiped them alone. But now that she was working so hard she needed the whole afternoon to get her lessons in, and insisted that Betty should help get supper and wipe dishes afterwards. For once Mrs. Gardiner took sides with Migwan and commanded Betty to do her share of the work. In consequence Betty developed a fierce resentment against Migwan's literary efforts, and taunted her continually with her failure to make anything of it. Since she had been working on Professor Green's book Migwan had done nothing at all in the house, and her usual Saturday work fell to Betty.

Mrs. Gardiner was not feeling well of late, and could do no sweeping, so Betty found herself with a good day's work ahead of her one Saturday morning. Instead of playing that the dirt was a host of evil sprits, as Migwan did, which she could vanquish with the aid of her magic broom, Betty went at it sullenly and with a firm determination to do as little as possible and get through just as quickly as she could. She made up her mind that when Migwan went to market in the afternoon she would go along with her in the automobile. So by going hastily over the surface of things she got through by three o'clock, and when Gladys called for Migwan, Betty came running out too, with her coat and hat on, dressed in her best dress.

"Where are you going?" asked Migwan.

"Along with you," answered Betty.

"I'm afraid we can't take you," said Migwan; "there isn't enough room."

"Oh, I'll squeeze in," said Betty lightly. Now seven girls with market baskets in addition to the driver are somewhat of a crowd, and there really was no room for Betty in the machine. Besides, Betty was a great tease and the girls dreaded to have her with them, so no one said a word of encouragement.

"You can't come, and that is all there is to it," said Migwan rather crossly. She was in a hurry to be off and get the marketing done. Betty stamped her foot, and snatching Migwan's market basket, she ran around the corner of the house with it. Migwan ran after her, and forcibly recovering the basket, hit Betty over the head with it several times. Then she jumped into the automobile and the driver started off, leaving Betty standing looking after the rapidly disappearing car and working herself into a terrible temper. She ran into the house and slammed the door with such a jar that the vases on the mantel rattled and threatened to fall down. She threw her hat and coat on the floor and stamped on them in a perfect fury. On the sitting room table lay the pages of the book which Migwan was making for Professor Green. The edges were already burned and they were ready to be pasted on the brown mat. Betty's eyes suddenly snapped when she saw them. Here was a fine chance to be revenged on Migwan. With an exclamation of triumph she seized the leaves, tore them in half and threw them into the grate, standing by until they were consumed to ashes, and laughing spitefully the while.

Migwan came in briskly with her basket of provisions. Betty looked up slyly from the book she was reading, but said not a word. Migwan went into the sitting room and Betty heard her moving around. "Mother," called Migwan up the stairway, "where did you put the pages of my book? I left them on the sitting room table."

"I didn't touch them," replied her mother; "I haven't been downstairs since you went out."

"Betty," said Migwan sternly, "did you hide my work?" Betty laughed mockingly, but made no reply. "Make haste and give them back," commanded Migwan. "I have no time to waste."

Betty still maintained a provoking silence and Migwan began looking through the table drawers for the missing leaves. Betty watched her with malicious glee. "You may look a while before you find them," she said meaningly; "they're hidden in a nice, safe place."

Migwan stood and faced her, exasperated beyond endurance. "Betty Gardiner," she said angrily, "stop this nonsense at once and tell me where those pages are!"

"Well, if you're really curious to know," answered Betty, smiling wickedly, "I'll tell you. They're there" and she pointed to the grate.

"Betty," gasped Migwan, turning white, "you don't mean that you've burned them?"

"That's what I do mean," said Betty coolly. "I'll show you if you can treat me like a baby."

Migwan stood as if turned to stone. She could hardly believe that those fair pages, which represented so many hours of patient work, had been swept away in one moment of passion. Blindly she turned, and putting on her wraps, walked from the house without a word. It seemed to her that Fate had decreed that nothing which she undertook should succeed. Discouragement settled down on her like a black pall. With the ability to do things which should set her above her fellows, she was being relentlessly pursued by some strange fatality which marked every effort of hers a failure. She walked aimlessly up street after street without any idea where she was going, entirely oblivious to her surroundings. Wandering thus, she discovered that she was in the park, and had come out on the high bluff of the lake. She stood moodily looking down at the vast field of ice that such a short time before had been tossing waves. The lake, to all appearances, was frozen solid out as far as the one-mile crib. There was a curious stillness in the air, as when the clock had stopped, due to the absence of the noise made by the waves dashing on the rocks. Nothing had ever appealed so to Migwan as did the absolute silence and solitude of that frozen lake. Her bruised young spirit was weary of contact with people, and found balm in this icy desert where there was so sound of a human voice. As far as the eye could see there was not a living being in sight. A skating carnival in the other end of the park drew the attention of all who were abroad on this Saturday afternoon, and kept them away from the lake front.

A desire to be enveloped in this solitude came over Migwan; to get her feet off the earth altogether. She half slid and half climbed down the cliff and walked out on the ice. Before her the grey horizon line stretched vast and unbroken, and she walked out toward it, lost in dreaming. Sometimes the floor under her feet was smooth and polished as a pane of glass, and sometimes it was rough and covered with hummocks where the water had frozen in the wind. In Migwan's fancy this was not the lake she was walking on; it was one of the great Swiss glaciers. Those grey clouds there, standing out against the black ones, they were the mountains, and she was taking her perilous journey through the mountain pass. The ice cracked slightly under her feet, but she did not notice. She was a Swiss guide, taking a party of tourists across the glacier. Underneath this floor of ice were the bodies of those travelers who had fallen into the crevices. She was telling the tourists the stories of the famous disasters and they were shuddering at her tale. The ice cracked again under her feet, but her mind, soaring in flights of fancy, took no heed.

Her imagination took another turn. Now she was Mrs. Knollys, in the famous story, waiting for the body of her husband to be given up by the glacier. The long years of waiting passed and she stood at the foot of the glacier watching the miracle unfold before her eyes. The glacier was making queer cracking noises as it descended, and it sounded as though there was water underneath it. She could hear it lapping.

C-R-A-C-K! A sound rang out on the still air that startled Migwan like the report of a pistol, followed immediately by another. She came to her senses with a rush. With hardly a moment's warning the ice on which she was standing broke away from the main mass and began to move. Struck motionless by fright, she had not the presence of mind to jump back to the larger field. A wave washed in between, separating her by several feet from the solid ice. The cake she was on began to heave and fall sickeningly. There was another cracking sound and the edge of the solid body of ice broke up into dozens of floating cakes, that ground and pounded each other as the waves set them in motion. Every drop of blood receded from Migwan's heart as she realized what had happened. She screamed aloud, once, and then knew the futility of it. Her voice could not reach to the shore. Lake and sky and horizon line now mocked her with their silence. The cake of ice, lurching and tipping, began floating out to sea.

On this wintry afternoon Sahwah left the house in a far different mood from that which had carried Migwan blindly over the ground. Her eyes were sparkling with the joy of life and her cheeks were glowing in the cold. She wore a heavy reefer sweater and a knitted cap. Under her arm was her latest plaything—a pair of skis. By her side walked Dick Albright, one of the boys in her class, whom she considered especially good fun. Dick also had a pair of skis. The two of them were bound for the park to practice "making descents" from the hillsides. Sahwah was absolutely happy, and chattered like one of the sparrows that were flocking on the lawns and streets. Her chief interest in life just now was the school basketball team, of which she was a member. Soon, very soon, would come the big game with the Carnegie Mechanics, which would decide the championship of the city. Sahwah was the star forward for the Washington High team, and it was no secret that the winning of that game depended upon her to a great extent. Sahwah was the idol of the athletically inclined portion of the school. Dick thought there never was such a player—for a girl.

Sahwah was full of basketball talk now, and made shrewd comments on the good and bad points of both teams, weighing the chances of each with great care. "Mechanicals' center is shorter than ours; we have the advantage there. One of their forwards is good and the other isn't, and one of our guards is weak. On the whole, we're about evenly matched."

"Fine chance Mechanicals'll have with you in the game," said Dick.

"The only thing I'm afraid of," said Sahwah, with a thoughtful pucker, "is Marie Lanning; you know, Joe Lanning's cousin. She's to guard me and she's a head taller."

"Don't worry, you'll manage all right," said Dick. Sahwah laughed. It was pleasant to be looked up to as the hope of the school. "If you only don't get sick," said Dick.

"Don't be afraid," answered Sahwah. "I won't get sick. But if I don't get my Physics notebook finished by the First of February I'll not be eligible for the game, and that's no joke. Fizzy said nobody would get a passing grade this month who didn't have that old notebook finished, and you know what that means."

"There really isn't any danger of your not getting it in, is there?" asked Dick breathlessly.

"Not if I keep at it," answered Sahwah, and Dick breathed easy again. To allow yourself to be declared ineligible for a game on account of studies when the school was depending on you to win that game would have been a crime too awful to contemplate.

The snow on the hills in the park had a hard crust, which made it just right for skiing. Sahwah and Dick made one descent after another, sometimes tripping over the point of a ski and landing in a sprawling heap, but more often sailing down in perfect form with a breathless rush. "That last leap of yours was a beauty," said Sahwah admiringly.

"I think I'm learning," said Dick modestly.

"I 'stump' you to go down the big hill on the lake front," said Sahwah, her eyes sparkling with mischief.

Dick knew what that particular hill was like, but, boylike, he could not refuse a dare given by a girl. "Do you want to see me do it?" he said stoutly. "All right, I will."

"Don't," said Sahwah, frightened at what she had driven him to do; "you'll break your neck. I didn't really mean to dare you to do it." But Dick had made up his mind to go down that cliff hill just to show Sahwah that he could, and nothing could turn him aside now.

"Come along," he said; "I can make it." And he started off toward the lake front at a brisk pace.

But when he had reached the top of the hill in question he stood still and stared out over the lake. "Hello," he said in surprise, "there's somebody having trouble out there on the ice." Sahwah came and stood beside him, shading her eyes with her hand to see what was happening. At that distance she did not recognize Migwan. "The ice is breaking!" cried Dick, who was far-sighted and saw the girl on the floating ice cake. Like a whirlwind he sped down the hillside, dropped over the edge of the cliff like a plummet and shot nearly a hundred feet out over the glassy surface of the lake. Without pausing an instant Sahwah was after him. She had a dizzy sensation of falling off the earth when she made the jump from the hillside, which was a greater distance than she had ever dropped before, but it was over so quickly that she had no time to lose her breath before she was on solid ground again and taking the long slide over the lake. In a short time they reached the edge of the broken ice.

"Migwan!" gasped Sahwah when she saw who the girl on the floating cake was. They could not get very near her, as the edge of the solid mass was continually breaking away, and there was a strip of moving pieces between them and her. "Fasten the skis together and make a long pole," said Sahwah, "and then she can take hold of one end of it and we can pull her toward us," said Sahwah.

"Good idea," said Dick, and proceeded to lash the long strips together with the straps, aided by sundry strings and handkerchiefs.

Then there were several moments of suspense until Migwan came within reach of the pole. She simply had to wait until she floated near enough to grasp it, which the perverse ice cake seemed to have no intention of doing.

The right combination of wind and wave came at last, however, and drove her in toward the shore. She was still beyond the end of the pole. "Jump onto the next cake," called Sahwah. Migwan obeyed in fear and trembling. It took still another jump before she could reach the lifesaver. She was now separated from the broken mass at the edge of the solid ice by about six feet. With Migwan clinging fast to the pole Dick began to pull in gently, so as not to pull her off the ice, and the cake began to move across this open space until it was close beside the nearer mass of broken pieces. Then, supported by the improvised hand rail, Migwan leaped from one cake to the next, and so made her way back to the solid part. It was an exciting process, for the pieces tipped and heaved when she stepped on them, and bobbed up and down, and some turned over just as her feet left them.

"Eliza crossing the ice," said Sahwah, giggling nervously.

Migwan sank down exhausted when she felt the solid mass under her feet and knew that the danger was over. She was chilled through and through, and more than one wave had splashed over the floating ice while she was on it and soaked her shoes and stockings. Sahwah took this in at a glance. "Get up," she said sharply, "and run. Run all the way home if you don't want to get pneumonia. It's your only chance." Taking hold of her hands, Dick and Sahwah ran along beside her, making her keep up the pace when she pleaded fatigue. More dead than alive she reached home, but warm from head to foot. Sahwah rolled her in hot blankets and administered hot drinks with a practiced hand. Neither Mrs. Gardiner nor Betty were at home. Migwan soon dropped off to sleep, and woke feeling entirely well. Thanks to Sahwah's taking her in hand she emerged from the experience without even a sign of a cold.

With heroic patience and courage she began again the weary task of typing and burning all the pages of Professor Green's book and finished it this time without mishap. The money she received for it all went into the family purse. Not a cent did she spend on herself.

Not long after this Migwan had a taste of fame. She had a poem printed in the paper! It happened in this way. At the Sunbeam Nursery one morning Nyoda saw her surrounded by a group of breathlessly listening children and joined the circle to hear the story Migwan was telling. She had apparently just finished, and the childish voices were calling out from all sides, "Tell it again!" Nyoda listened with interest as Migwan, with a solemn expression and impressive voice, recited the tragic tale of the "Goop Who Wouldn't Wash":

  Gunther Augustus Agricola Gunn,

He was a Goop if there ever was one!

Slapped his small sister whene'er he could reach her,

Muddied the carpet, made mouths at the preacher,

Talked back to his mother whenever she chid,

Always did otherwise than he was bid;

Gunther Augustus Agricola Gunn,

Manners he certainly had not a one!

O bad little Goops, wheresoe'er you may be,

Take heed what befell young Agricola G!

For Gunther Augustus (unlike you, I hope),

Had an inborn aversion to water and soap;

He fought when they washed him, he squirmed and he twisted,

He shrieked, scratched and wriggled until they desisted;

He would not be combed—it was no use to try—

O he was a Goop, they could all testify!

So Gunther went dirty—unwashed and uncombed,

With hands black as pitch through the garden he roamed;

When suddenly a monstrous black shadow fell o'er him,

And the Woman Who Scrubs Dirty Goops stood before him!

Her waist was a washcloth, her skirt was a towel,

She looked down at him with a horrible scowl;

One hand was a brush and the other a comb,

Her forehead was soap and her pompadour foam!

Her foot was a shoebrush, and on it did grow

A shiny steel nail file in place of a toe!

Gunther Augustus Agricola Gunn,

He had a fright if he ever had one!

In a twinkling she seized him—Oh, how he did shriek!

And threw him headforemost right into the creek!

Rubbed soap in his eyes (Dirty Goops, O beware!),

And in combing the snarls pulled out handfuls of hair!

Scrubbed the skin off his nose, brushed his teeth till they bled,

Tweaked his ears, rapped his knuckles, and gleefully said,

"Gunther Augustus Agricola Gunn,

There'll be a difference when I get done!"

After that young Agricola strove hard to see

How very, how heavenly good he could be!

Wiped his feet at the door, tipped his hat to the preacher,

Caressed his small sister whene'er he could reach her!

Stood still while they washed him and combed out his hair,

His garments he folded and laid on a chair!

Gunter Augustus Agricola Gunn,

He was a saint if there ever was one!

"Where did you get that poem?" asked Nyoda.

"I wrote it myself," answered Migwan.

"Good work!" said Nyoda; "will you give me a copy?"

Nyoda showed the poem to Professor Green and Professor Green showed it to a friend who was column editor of one of the big dailies, and one fine morning the poem appeared in the paper, with Migwan's full name and address at the bottom, "Elsie Gardiner, Adams Ave." The Gardiners did not happen to take that particular paper and Migwan knew nothing of it until she reached school and was congratulated on all sides. Professor Green, who had taken a great interest in Migwan since she had worked up his hunting notes in such a striking style, and regarded her as his special protégé, was anxious to have the whole school know what a gifted girl she was. He had a conference with the principal, and as a result Migwan was asked to read her poem at the rhetorical exercises in the auditorium that day. When she finished the applause was deafening, and with blushing cheeks and downcast eyes she ran from the stage. There were distinguished visitors at school that day, representatives of a national organization who had come to address the scholars, and they came up to Migwan after she had read her poem to be introduced and offer congratulations. Teachers stopped her in the hall to tell her how bright she was, and the other pupils regarded her with great respect. Migwan was the lion of the hour.

She hurried home on flying feet and danced into the house waving the paper. "Oh, mother," she called, as soon as she was inside the door, "guess what I've got to show you!" Her mother was not in the kitchen and she ran through the house looking for her. "Oh, mother," she called, "oh, moth— why, what's the matter?" she asked, stopping in surprise in the sitting room door. Mrs. Gardiner lay on the couch, and beside her sat the family doctor. Betty stood by looking very much frightened. Mrs. Gardiner looked up as Migwan came in. "It's nothing," she said, trying to speak lightly; "just a little spell."

"Mother has to go to the hospital," said Betty in a scared voice.

"Just a little operation," said Mrs. Gardiner hastily, as Migwan looked ready to drop. "Nothing serious—very."

Migwan's hour of triumph was completely forgotten in the anxiety of the next few days. Her mother rallied slowly from the operation, and it looked as though she would have to remain in the hospital a long time. It was impossible to meet this added expense from their little income, and Migwan, setting her teeth bravely, drew the remainder of her college money from the bank to pay the hospital and surgeon's bills. Then she set to work with redoubled zeal to write something which would sell. So far everything she had sent out had come back promptly. For a long time certain advertisements in the magazines had been holding her attention. They read something like this: "Write Moving Picture Plays. Bring $50 to $100 each. We teach you how by an infallible method. Anybody can do it. Full particulars sent for a postage stamp." Migwan had seen quite a few picture plays, many of them miserably poor, and felt that she could write better ones than some, or at least just as good. She wrote to the address given in one of the advertisements, asking for "full particulars." Back came a letter couched in the most glowing terms, which Migwan was not experienced enough to recognize as a multigraphed copy, which stated that the writer had noticed in her letter of inquiry a literary ability well worth cultivating, and he would feel himself highly honored to be allowed to teach her to write moving picture plays, a field in which she would speedily gain fame and fortune. He would throw open the gates of success for her for the nominal fee of thirty dollars, with five dollars extra for "stationery, etc." His regular fee was thirty-five dollars, but it was not often that he came across so much ability as she had, and he considered the pleasure he would derive from the correspondence course worth five dollars to him. Would she not send the first payment of five dollars by return mail so that his enjoyment might begin as soon as possible?

Migwan read the letter through with a beating heart until she came to the price, when her heart sank into her shoes. To pay thirty dollars was entirely out of the question. She wrote to several more advertisements and received much the same answer from all of them. There was only one which she could consider at all. This one offered no correspondence course, but advertised a book giving all the details of scenario writing, "history of the picture play, form, where to sell your plays, etc., all in one comprehensive volume." The price of the book was three dollars. Migwan hesitated a long time over this last one, but the subtle language of the advertisement drew her back again and again like a magnet, and finally overcame her doubts. "It will pay for itself many times when I have learned to write plays," she reflected. So she took three precious dollars from the housekeeping money and sent for the book. She did not ask Nyoda's advice this time; somehow she shrank from telling her about it.

In three days the book arrived. The "comprehensive volume" was a paper-covered pamphlet containing exactly twenty-nine pages. It could not have sold for more than ten or fifteen cents in a book store. The first five pages were devoted to a description of the phenomenal sale of the first edition of the book, two more enlarged upon the "unfillable demand" of the motion picture companies for scenarios, while the remainder of the book was given over to the "technique" of scenario writing. Migwan read it through eagerly, and did gain an idea of the form in which a play should be cast, although the information was meagre enough. Three dollars was an outrageous price to pay for the book, thought Migwan, but she comforted herself with the thought that by means of it she would soon lift the family out of their difficulties. She set to work with a cheery heart. Writing picture plays was easier than writing stories on account of the skeleton form in which they were cast, which made it unnecessary to strive for excellence of literary style. She finished the first one in two nights and sent it off with high hopes. The company she sent it to was listed in the book as "greatly in need of one-reel scenarios, and taking about everything sent to them." She was filled with a secret elation and went about the house singing like a lark, until Betty, who had been moping like an owl since her mother went to the hospital, was quite cheered up. "What are you so happy about?" she asked curiously. "You act as if somebody had left you a fortune."

"Maybe they have," replied Migwan mysteriously; "wait and see!"

Her joy was short-lived, however, for the play came back even more promptly than the stories had. Undaunted, she sent it out again and again. The reasons given for rejection would have been amusing if Migwan had not felt so disappointed. One said there was insufficient plot; one said the plot was too complicated; one said it was too long for a one-reel, and the next said it was too short even for a split-reel. Two places kept the return postage she had enclosed and sent the manuscript back collect. Scenario writing became a rather expensive amusement, instead of a bringer of fortune. In spite of all this, she kept on writing scenarios, for the fascination of the game had her in its grip, and she would never be satisfied until she succeeded. Lessons were thrust into the background of her mind by the throng of "scene-plots," "leaders," "bust-scenes," "inserts," "synopses," etc., that flashed through her head continually.

To write steadily night after night, after the lessons had been gotten out of the way, was a great tax on her young strength. Nyoda was inflexible about her stopping typewriting at nine o'clock, but she went home and wrote by hand until midnight. Nyoda was over at the house one afternoon when Migwan was settling down to get her lessons, and saw her take a dose from a phial.

"What are you taking medicine for?" she asked.

"Oh, this is just something to tone me up," replied Migwan.

"What is it?" insisted Nyoda.

"It's strychnine," said Migwan.

"Strychnine!" said Nyoda in a horrified voice. "Who taught you to take strychnine as a stimulant?"

"Mabel Collins did," answered Migwan. "She said she always took it when she had a dance on for every night in the week and couldn't keep up any other way, and it made her feel fine." Mabel Collins belonged to what the class called the "fast bunch."

"I'll have a talk with Mabel Collins," said Nyoda with a resolute gleam in her eye. "And, remember, no more of this 'tonic' for you. I knew girls in college who took strychnine to keep themselves going through examinations or other occasions of great physical strain, and they have suffered for it ever since. If you are doing so much that you can't 'keep up' any other way than by taking powerful medicines, it is time you 'kept down.' Fresh air and regular sleep are all the tonic you need. You stay away from that typewriter for a whole week and go to bed at nine o'clock every night. I'm coming down to tuck you in. Now remember!" And with this solemn warning Nyoda left her.

CHAPTER VIII.

SAHWAH MAKES A BASKET.

The game between the Washington High School and the Carnegie Mechanics Institute, which was to decide the girls' basketball championship of the city, was scheduled for the 15th of February. Up until this year Washington High had never come within sight of the championship. Then this season something had happened to the Varsity team which had made it a power to be reckoned with among the schools of the city. That something was Sahwah. Thanks to her playing, Washington High had not lost a single game so far. Her being put on the team was purely due to chance. Sahwah was a Junior and the Varsity team were all Seniors. She was a member of the "scrub" or practice team and an ardent devotee of the sport. During one of the early games of the season Sahwah was sitting on the side lines attentively watching every bit of play.

The game was going against the Washington, due to the fact that their forwards were too slow to break through the guarding of the rival team. Sahwah saw the weakness and tingled with a desire to get into the game and do some speed work. As by a miracle the chance was given her. One of the forwards strained her finger slightly and was taken from the game. Her substitute, who had been sitting next to Sahwah, had left her seat and gone to the other end of the gymnasium. The instructor, who was acting as referee, in her excitement mistook Sahwah for the substitute and called her out on the floor. Sahwah wondered but obeyed instantly and went into the game as forward. Then the spectators began to sit up and take notice. Sahwah had not been two minutes on the floor when she made a basket right between the arms of the tall guard. The ripple of surprise had hardly died away before she had made another. Then the baskets followed thick and fast. In five minutes of play she had tied the score. The guards could hardly believe their eyes when they saw this lithe girl slipping like an eel through their defense and caging the ball with a sure hand every time. The game ended with an overwhelming victory for the Washingtons and there was a new star forward on the horizon. Sahwah was changed from the practice team to the Varsity.

From that time forward Washington High forged steadily ahead in the race for the championship and as yet had no defeat on its record. However, Washington had a formidable rival in the Carnegie Mechanics Institute, which was also undefeated so far. The Mechanicals were slightly older girls and were known as a whirlwind team. Sahwah, who foresaw long ago that the supreme struggle would be between the Washingtons and the Mechanicals, attended the games played by the Mechanicals whenever she could and studied their style of playing. "Star players, every one," was her deduction, "but weak on team work." Sahwah was not so dazzled by her own excellence as a player that she could not recognize greatness in a rival, and she readily admitted that one of the girls who guarded for the Mechanicals was the best guard she had ever seen. This was Marie Lanning, whose cousin Joe was in Sahwah's class at Washington High. Sahwah knew instinctively that when the struggle came she would go up against this girl. The game would really be between these two. Washington's hope lay in Sahwah's ability to make baskets, and the hope of the Mechanicals was Marie's ability to keep her from making them. So she studied Marie's guarding until she knew the places where she could break through.

Marie Lanning also knew that it was Sahwah she would have to deal with. But there was a difference in the attitude of the girls toward each other. Sahwah regarded Marie as her opponent, but she respected her prowess. She had no personal resentment against Marie for being a good guard; she looked upon her as an enemy merely because she belonged to a rival school. Marie on the other hand actually hated Sahwah. Before Sahwah appeared on the scene she had been the greatest player in the Athletic Association, the heroine of every game. She was pointed out everywhere she went as "Marie Lanning, the basketball player." Now some of her glory was dimmed, for another star had risen, Sarah Ann Brewster, the whirlwind forward of the Washington High team, was threatening to overshadow her. It was a distinctly personal matter with her. Sahwah wanted to win that game so her school would have the championship; Marie wanted to win it for her own glory. She did not really believe that Sahwah was as great as she was made out. It was only because she had never run against a great guard that she had been able to roll up the score for Washington so many times. Well, she would find out a thing or two when she played the Mechanicals, Marie reflected complacently. She had never seen Sahwah play, and if any one had suggested that it would be a good thing to watch her tactics she would have been very scornful. She was confident in her own powers.

Then there came a rather important game of Washington High's on a night when Marie was visiting her cousin Joe. He had tickets for the game and took her along. Now for the first time she beheld her foe. After watching Sahwah's marvelous shots at the basket and the confusion of the girl who was guarding her, Marie began to feel uneasy. It now seemed to her that Sahwah's powers had been underestimated in the reports instead of over-estimated. The game ended just as all the others had done, with a great score for Washington High and Sahwah the idol of the hour. Marie looked on with a slight sneer when Sahwah, after the game was over, frankly congratulated the losing team on their playing, which had been pretty good throughout. "Do you know," said Sahwah straightforwardly, "that if you had had a little better team work, I don't believe we could have beaten you."

"Any day we could have won with you in the game," said one of the losers, "the way you can shoot that ball into the basket."

Without being at all puffed up by this compliment, Sahwah proceeded to make her point. "My throwing the ball into the basket wasn't what won the game," she said simply, "it was the fact that I had it to throw. It's all due to the girls who see that I get it. It's team work that wins every time and not individual starring." Thus was Sahwah in the habit of disclaiming the credit of victory.

Joe brought up Marie Lanning and introduced her. "So this is my deadly enemy," said Sahwah pleasantly. Marie acknowledged the introduction politely, but while her lips smiled her eyes had a steely glitter. Sahwah was surrounded by a crowd of admiring friends at this time and there was no chance for further conversation, and she did not become aware of Marie's animosity. "We'll meet again," Sahwah said meaningly, with a pleasant laugh, as Marie and Joe turned to go. "That is," she added with a humorous twinkle, "if I don't go down in my studies and get myself debarred from playing."

"Fine chance of your going down," said Joe.

"Oh, I don't know," laughed Sahwah; "it all depends on whether I get my Physics notebook in by the First." A shout of laughter greeted this remark. The idea of Sahwah's getting herself debarred on account of her studies was too funny for words.

"Well," said Joe to Marie when they were outside the building, "that's the girl you're going to have to play against. What do you think of her?" In his heart Joe thought that his cousin Marie would have no trouble holding Sahwah down.

"She's a great deal faster than I thought," said Marie with a thoughtful frown.

"But you can beat her, can't you?" asked Joe anxiously. "You've got to. I've staked my whole winter's allowance that you would win the championship."

"I didn't know that you were in the habit of betting," said Marie a little disdainfully.

"I never did before," said Joe, "but some of the fellows were saying that nobody could hold out against that Brewster girl and I said I bet my cousin could, and so we talked back and forth until I offered to bet real money on you."

Marie was flattered at this, as her kind would be. "I can beat her," she said, but there was fear in her heart. "Oh, if she would only be debarred from the game!" she exclaimed eagerly.

But Sahwah had no intentions of being put out on that score. She applied herself assiduously to the making of the notebook that was required as the resume of the half year's work. She finished it a whole day ahead of time, and then, Sahwah-like, was so pleased with herself that she decided to celebrate the event. "Come over to the house to-night," she said to various of her girl and boy friends in school that day. "I'm entertaining in honor of my Physics notebook!"

When the guests arrived the notebook was enthroned on a gilded easel on the parlor table and decorated with a wreath of flowers and a card bearing the inscription "Endlich!" The very ridiculousness of the whole affair was enough to make every one have a good time. The Winnebagos were there, and some of their brothers and cousins, and Dick Albright and Joe Lanning and several more boys from the class. Naturally much of the conversation turned on the coming game, and Sahwah was solemnly assured that she would forfeit their friendship forever if she did not win the championship for the school. School spirit ran high and songs and yells were practiced until the neighbors groaned. Joe Lanning joined in the yells with as much vigor as any. No one knew that he was secretly on the side of the Mechanicals.

Sahwah's notebook came in for inspection and much admiration, for she was good at Physics and her drawings were to be envied. "I see you have a list of all the problems the class has done this year," said Dick Albright, looking through the notebook. "Do you mind if I copy them from your list? I lost the one Fizzy gave us in class and it'll take me all night to pick them out from the ones in the book."

"Certainly, you may," said Sahwah cordially. "Take it along with you and bring it to school in the morning. It'll be all right as long as I get it in by that time. But don't forget it, whatever you do, unless you want to see me put out of the game." Joe Lanning wished fervently that Dick would forget to bring it. The party broke up and the boys and girls prepared to depart.

"What car do you take, Dick?" asked one of the boys.

"I don't think I'll take any," said Dick. "I'll just run around the corner with this lady," he said, indicating Migwan, "and then I'll walk the rest of the way."

"Isn't it pretty far?" asked some one else.

"Not the way I go," answered Dick. "I take the short cut through the railway tunnel." Joe Lanning's eyes gleamed suddenly.

The good-nights were all said and Sahwah shut the door and set the furniture straight before she went to bed. "Didn't your friends stay rather late?" asked her mother from upstairs.

"No," said Sahwah, "I don't think so, it's only—why, the clock has stopped," she finished after a look at the mantel, "I don't know what time it is."

"Get the time from the telephone operator," said her mother, "and set the clock."

Sahwah picked up the receiver. There was a strange buzzing noise on the wire. "Zig-a-zig, ziz-zig-zig-a-zig, zig-g-g, zig-g-g, zig-g-g-g." Puzzled at first, she soon recognized what it was. It was the sound of Joe Lanning's wireless. Joe lived directly back of Sahwah on the next street, and the aerial of his wireless apparatus was fastened to the telephone pole in the Brewsters' yard. Joe was "sending," and the vibrations were being picked up by the telephone wires and carried to her ear when she had the receiver down. Sahwah understood the wireless code the boys used, and, in fact, had both sent and received messages. She knew it was Joe's custom to listen for the time every night as it was flashed out from the station at Arlington, and then send it to his friend Abraham Goldstein, a young Jewish lad in the class, who also had a wireless. Then the two would send each other messages and verify them the next day. "Oh, what fun," thought Sahwah; "I can get Arlington time to-night." She asked the operator to look up a new number for her to keep her off the line and then got out paper and pencil to take down the message as it went out. As she deciphered it she gasped in astonishment. She had expected a message something on this order: "Hello, Abraham—how are you?—Arlington says ten bells—How's the weather in your neck of the woods?" Instead the words were entirely different. She could not believe her eyes as she made them out. "Albright going through railway tunnel—hold him up—get notebook away—keep Brewster out of game." Her senses reeled as she understood the meaning of the message. That Joe was plotting against her when he pretended to be a friend cut her to the quick. For a moment her lip quivered; then her nature asserted itself. There was a thing to do and she must do it. Dick must be kept from going through the tunnel. Turning out the lights downstairs, she crept noiselessly out of the house, found her brother's bicycle on the porch and pedaled off after Dick. She knew exactly the way he would take. From Migwan's house he would go up Adams to Locust Street and from there to ——th Avenue, and keep on going until he came to the dark tunnel. Sahwah nearly burst with indignation when she thought of Joe's cowardly conduct. He was calmly getting Abraham to do the dirty work for him, so he would never be suspected of having anything to do with it in case Dick recognized Abraham. She could see how the thing would work out. Abraham lived just the other side of the tunnel. All he would have to do would be to stand in the shadow of the tunnel, jump out on Dick as he came through, seize the notebook from his hand, and run away before Dick knew what had happened. There would be no need of fighting or hurting him. But Joe's end would be accomplished and Washington would lose the game. The fact that he was a traitor to the school hurt Sahwah ten times worse than the injury he was trying to do her. "Even if his cousin is on the other side, he belongs to Washington," she repeated over and over to herself.

Down Locust Street she flew and along deserted ——th Avenue. It was bitterly cold riding, but she took no notice. Far ahead of her she could see Dick walking briskly toward the fatal tunnel. Pedaling for dear life she caught up with him when he was still some distance from it. "Whatever is the matter?" he asked, startled, as she flung herself breathless from the wheel beside him.

"The notebook," she said. "Joe's trying to get it away from you. He's got Abraham Goldstein waiting in the tunnel to snatch it as you go by."

Dick gave vent to a long whistle of astonishment. "Of all the underhand tricks!" he exclaimed when the full significance of Joe's act was borne in on him. He was stupefied to think that Joe was a traitor to the school. "That'll fix his chances of getting into the Thessalonians," he said vehemently. "His name is coming up next week to be voted on. Just wait until I tell what I know about him!"

Dick retraced his steps and took Sahwah home, where he left the precious notebook in her keeping to prevent any possibility of its getting lost before she could hand it in, and then took the streetcar and rode home the roundabout way, arriving there in safety. Abraham waited out in the cold tunnel for several hours and then gave it up and went home, feeling decidedly out of temper with Joe Lanning and his intrigues.

The game was held in the Washington High gymnasium. The gallery and all available floor space were packed long before the commencement of the game. The Carnegie Mechanics came out in a body to witness their team win the championship. Joe Lanning was there, entirely composed, though inwardly raging at the failure of his trick, which he attributed to Dick's changing his mind about walking home, never dreaming that Sahwah had intercepted his message and his treachery was known. Although his sympathies were with the Mechanicals he stood with the Washingtons and yelled their yells as loudly as any. The Mechanicals, as the visiting, team, came out on the floor first and had the first practice. They were fine looking girls, every one of them, with their dazzling white middies and blue ties. They were greeted with a ringing cheer from their rooters:

"Me-chan-i, Me-chan-i, Me-chan-i-can-can, Me-chan-i-can-can, Me-chan-i-cals!"

Marie Lanning held up her head and looked self-conscious when she heard the familiar yell thundered at the team. It was meant mostly for herself, she was sure. She smiled proudly and graciously in the direction whence the yell had proceeded. Quiet had hardly fallen on the crowd when there was heard the sound of singing from the upper end of the gymnasium where the door to the dressing rooms was. The tune was "Old Black Joe":

  "We're coming, we're coming,

  Star players, every one,

  We're going to win the championship

  For Washington!"

Washington's rooters caught up the yell and made the roof ring. Sahwah's heart swelled when she heard it, not with the feeling that they were singing to her, but with pride because she belonged to a team which called out this expression of loyalty. Then came individual cheers, with her name at the head of the list.

  "One, two, three, four,

  Who are we for?

  BREWSTER!"

Not even then was Sahwah puffed up.

The Washington High team wore black bloomers and red ties; they were a brilliant sight as they marched in with their hands on each other's shoulders. The teams took their places; a hush fell on the crowd; the referee's whistle sounded; the ball went up. Washington's center knocked it toward her basket; Sahwah, darting out from under the basket, caught it, sent it flying back to center; center threw it to the other Washington forward; Sahwah jumped directly behind Marie Lanning, received the ball from the other forward and shot the basket. Time, one minute from the sending up of the ball. The Washington team machine was working splendidly. A deafening roar greeted the first score. Marie bit her lip angrily. She had vowed to keep Washington from scoring. But Sahwah had not watched Marie play for nothing. She saw that she put up a wonderful guard when confronting her girl, but she was not always quick in turning around. Sahwah's plan of action was to keep away from her as much as possible and to get hold of the ball when she was behind Marie's back and throw for the basket before Marie could turn around. Guarding is only effective when you have some one to guard and Marie discovered she was really playing a game of tag with Sahwah, who was continually running away from her. With the wonderful team work which the Washington team had developed and their perfect understanding of each other's movements, Sahwah could get widely separated from Marie and be sure to receive the ball at just the right moment to throw a basket. Twice she made it; three times; four times. Pandemonium reigned. "Guard her, Marie!" shrieked the Mechanicals.

The score stood 8 to in favor of Washington at the end of the first five minutes. Marie was white with rage. Was this a girl she was trying to guard, or was it an eel? She would get her cornered with the ball, Sahwah would measure Marie's height with her eye, locate the basket with a brief glance, stiffen her muscles for a jump, and then as Marie stood ready to beat down the ball, as it rose in the air, Sahwah would suddenly relax, twist into some inconceivable position, shoot the ball low to center and be a dozen feet away before Marie could get her hands down from the air.

"B-R-E, DOUBLE-U, S, T-E-R, BREWSTER!"

sang the Washington rooters in ecstasy. It was maddening. There was no hope of keeping her from scoring. The time came when Sahwah and Marie both had their hands on the ball at the same time and it called for a toss-up. As the ball rose in the air Marie struck out as if to send it flying to center, but instead of that, her hand, clenched, with a heavy ring on one finger, struck Sahwah full on the nose. It was purely accidental, as every one could see. Sahwah staggered back dizzily, seeing stars. Her nose began to bleed furiously. She was taken from the game and her substitute put in. A groan went up from the Washington students as she was led out, followed by a suppressed cheer from the Carnegie Mechanics. Marie met Joe's eye with a triumphant gleam in her own.

Sahwah was beside herself at the thing which had happened to her. The game and the championship were lost to Washington. The hope of the team was gone. The girl who took her place was far inferior, both in skill in throwing the ball and in tactics. She could not make a single basket. The score rolled up on the Mechanicals' side; now it was tied. Sahwah, trying to stanch the blood that flowed in a steady stream, heard the roar that followed the tying of the score and ground her teeth in misery. The Mechanicals were scoring steadily now. The first half ended 12 to 8 in their favor. But if Marie had expected to be the heroine of the game now that Sahwah was out of it she was disappointed. The girl who had taken Sahwah's place required no skilful guarding; she would not have made any baskets anyhow, and there was no chance for a brilliant display of Marie's powers. Marie stood still on the floor after the first half ended, listening to the cheers and expecting her name to be shouted above the rest, but nothing like that happened. The yells were for the team in general, while the Washingtons, loyal to Sahwah to the last, cheered her to the echo.

The noise penetrated to the dressing room where she lay on a mat:

"Ach du lieber lieber,

Ach du lieber lieber,

BREWSTER! No, ja, bum bum!

Ach du lieber lieber,

Ach du lieber lieber,

BREWSTER! No, ja!"

Sahwah raised her head. Another cheer rent the air:

"B-R-E, DOUBLE-U, S, T-E-R, BREWSTER!"

Sahwah sat up.

"BREWSTER! BREWSTER! WE WANT BREWSTER!" thundered the gallery. Sahwah sprang to her feet. Like a knight of old, who, expiring on the battlefield, heard the voice of his lady love and recovered miraculously, Sahwah regained her strength with a rush when she heard the voice of her beloved school calling her.

When the teams came out for the second half Sahwah came out with them. The gallery rocked with the joy of the Washingtonians. The whistle sounded; the ball went up; the machine was in working order again. Washington was jubilant; Carnegie Mechanics was equally confident now that it was in the lead. Sahwah played like a whirlwind. She shot the ball into the basket right through Marie's hands. Once! Twice! The score was again tied. "12 to 12," shouted the scorekeeper through her megaphone. Like the roar of the waves of the sea rose the yell of the Washingtonians:

"Who tied the score when the score was rolling?

Who tied the score when the score was rolling?

Brewster, yes?

Well, I guess!

She tied the score when the score was rolling!"

Then Sahwah's luck turned and she could make no more baskets. She began to feel weak again and fumbled the ball more than once. Marie laughed sneeringly when Sahwah failed to score on a foul. The game was drawing to a close. "Two more minutes to play!" called the referee. The ball was under the Mechanicals' basket. The Washington guards got possession of it and passed it forward to Sahwah, who threw for the basket and missed. The ball came down right in the hands of Marie. The Mechanicals were excellently placed to pass it by several stages down to their basket. Instead of throwing it to center, however, she tried to make a grandstand play and threw it the entire length of the gymnasium to the waiting forward. It fell short and there was a wild scramble to secure it. Washington got it. "One minute to play!" called the referee. A score must be made now by one side or the other or the game would end in a tie. The Washington guard located Sahwah. The Mechanicals closed in around her so that she could not get away by herself. Marie towered over her triumphantly. At last had come the chance to use her famous method of guarding. The crowd in the gallery leaned forward, tense and silent. The Mechanicals' forwards ran back under their basket to be in position to throw the ball in when Marie should send it down to them. The Washington guard threw the ball toward the massed group in the center of the floor. As a tiger leaps to its prey, Sahwah, with a mighty spring, jumped high in the air and caught the ball over the heads of the blocking guards. Before the Mechanicals had recovered from their surprise she sent it whirling toward the distant basket. It rolled around the rim, hesitated for one breathless instant and then dropped neatly through the netting. It was a record throw from the field.

"Time's up," called the referee.

"Score, 14 to 12 in favor of Washington High," shouted the scorekeeper.

The pent-up emotions of the Washington rooters found vent in a prolonged cheer; then the crowd surged across the floor and surrounded Sahwah, and she was borne in triumph from the gymnasium.

Joe Lanning and his cousin Marie, avoiding the merry throng, left the building with long faces and never a word to say.

CHAPTER IX.

THE THESSALONIAN PLAY.

It was the custom each year for the Thessalonians, the Boys' Literary Society of Washington High School, to give a play in the school auditorium. This year the play was to be a translation of Briand's four-act drama, "Marie Latour." After a careful consideration of the talents of their various girl friends, Gladys was asked to play the leading role and Sahwah was also given a part in the cast. It was the play where the unfortunate Marie Latour, pursued by enemies, hides her child in a hollow statue of Joan of Arc. In order to produce the piece a large statue of the Maid of Orleans was made to order. It was constructed of some inexpensive composition and painted to look like bronze. In the one scene a halo appears around the head of the Maid while she is sheltering the child. This effect was produced by a circle of tiny lights worked by a storage battery inside the statue. For the sake of convenience in installing the electric apparatus and the wiring, one half of the skirt—it was the statue representing Joan in woman's clothes, not the one in armor—was made in the form of a door, which opened on hinges. The base of the statue was of wood. It was not finished until the day before the play and was used for the first time at the dress rehearsal, when it was left standing on the stage.

Joe Lanning was in rather a dark mood these days. In the first place, he had lost his winter's allowance of pocket money by staking it on the Washington-Carnegie Mechanics game. After this he was treated coolly by a large number of his classmates, and, not knowing that the story of his treachery was being privately circulated around the school, he could not guess the reason. The keenest desire of his life was to be made a member of the Thessalonian Literary Society, and if he had kept his record unsmirched he would have been taken in at the February election. He confidently expected to be elected, and was already planning in his mind the things he would do and say at the meetings, and what girls he would take to the Thessalonian dances. He received a rude shock when the election came and went and he was not taken in. He knew from reliable sources that his name was coming up to be voted on, and it was not very flattering to realize that he had been blackballed. From an eager interest in all Thessalonian doings his feeling changed to bitter resentment against the society. Just now the Thessalonian play was the topic of the hour, and the very mention of it almost made him ill. If he had been elected he would have been an usher at the play with the other new members and worn the club colors in his buttonhole to be admired by the girls and envied by the other fellows. But now there was none of that charmed fellowship for him. He nourished his feeling of bitterness and hatred until his scheming mind began to grope for some way of spoiling the success of the play. As usual, he turned to his friend, Abraham Goldstein, who was about the only one who had not shown any coolness. Together they watched their chance. The play progressed toward perfection, the dress rehearsal had been held, the day of the "First Night" had arrived. The stage was set and the statue of the Maid of Orleans was in place. Joe, poking around the back of the stage, saw the statue and received his evil inspiration.

Just about the time the play was given there was being held in the school an exhibition of water-color paintings. A famous and very valuable collection had been loaned by a friend of the school for the benefit of the students of drawing. The paintings were on display in one of the girls' club rooms on the fourth floor of the building. Hinpoha took great pleasure in examining them and spent a long time over them every day after school was closed. On the day of the play she went up as usual to the club room for an hour before going home. Reluctantly she tore herself away when she realized that the afternoon was passing. As she returned to the cloakroom where her wraps were she was surprised to find Emily Meeks there. Emily started guiltily when Hinpoha entered and made a desperate effort to finish wrapping up something she had in her hand. But her nervousness got into her fingers and made them tremble so that the object she held fell to the floor. As it fell the wrapper came open and Hinpoha could see what it was. It was one of the water colors of the exhibition collection, one of the smallest and most exquisite ones. Hinpoha gasped with astonishment when she caught Emily in the act of stealing it. Emily Meeks was the last person in the world Hinpoha would ever have accused of stealing anything.

Emily turned white and red by turns and leaned against the wall trembling. "Yes, I stole it," she said in a kind of desperation.

Something in her voice took the scorn out of Hinpoha's face. She looked at her curiously. "Why did you try to steal, Emily?" she asked gently.

Emily burst into tears and sank to her knees. "You wouldn't understand," she sobbed.

"Maybe I would," said Hinpoha softly, "try it and see."

Haltingly Emily told her tale. In a moment's folly she had promised to buy a set of books from an agent and had signed a paper pledging herself to pay for it within three months. The price was five dollars. At the time she thought she could save enough out of her meager wages to pay it, but found that she could not. The time was up several months ago and the agent was threatening her with a lawsuit if she did not pay up this month. Fearing that the people with whom she lived would be angry if they heard of the affair and would turn her out of her home into the streets—for to her a lawsuit was something vague and terrible and she thought she would have to go to jail when it was found she could not pay—she grew desperate, and being alone in the room with the paintings for an instant she had seized the opportunity and carried one out under her middy blouse. She intended to sell it and pay for the books.

Hinpoha's eyes filled with tears at Emily's distress. She was very tender hearted and was easily touched by other people's troubles. "If I lent you five dollars to pay for the books, would you take it?" she asked.

Emily started up like a condemned prisoner who is pardoned on the way to execution. "I'll pay it back," she cried, "if I have to go out scrubbing to earn the money. And you won't say anything about the picture," she said, clasping her hands beseechingly, "if I put it back where I got it?"

"No," said Hinpoha, with all the conviction of her loyal young nature,

"I give you my word of honor that I will never say anything about it."

"Oh, you're an angel straight from heaven," exclaimed Emily.

"First time I've heard of a red-headed angel," laughed Hinpoha.

Emily stooped to pick up the painting and restore it to its place, when she caught her breath in dismay. She had dropped a tear on the picture and made a light spot on the dark brown trunk of a tree. It was conspicuously noticeable, and would be sure to call forth the strictest inquiry. Emily covered her face with her hands. "It's my punishment," she groaned, "for trying to steal. Now I've ruined the honor of the school. We promised to send those pictures back unharmed if Mr. White would let us have them." Her dismay was intense.

Hinpoha examined the spot carefully. "Do you know," she said, "I believe I could fill in that place with dark color so it would never be noticed? The bark of the tree has a rough appearance and the slight unevenness around the edges of the spot will never be noticed. Don't worry, all will yet be well." If Hinpoha would have let her, Emily would have gone down on her knees to her. "Come, we must make haste," said Hinpoha. "You go right home and I will take the picture into our club room and fix it up and then slip upstairs with it and nobody will ever be any the wiser. It's a good thing there's nobody up there now."

Emily took her departure, vowing undying gratitude to Hinpoha, and Hinpoha took her paints from her desk and went into her own club room, which was on the third floor, and with infinite pains matched the shade of the tree trunk and repaired the damage. Her efforts were crowned with better success even than she had hoped for, and with thankfulness in her heart at the talent which could thus be turned to account to help a friend out of trouble, she surveyed the little painting, looking just as it did when loaned to the school. She carried it carefully upstairs, but at the door of the exhibition room she paused in dismay. A whole group of teachers and their friends were looking at the paintings and it was impossible to put the one back without being noticed. Irresolutely she turned away and retraced her steps to the third floor, intending to wait in her club room until the coast was clear. But alas! In coming out Hinpoha had left the door open. The club rooms were generally kept locked. While she was going upstairs a number of students coming out from late practice in the gymnasium spied the open door and went in to look around. It was impossible for Hinpoha to go in there with that picture in her hand. The only thing to do if she did not wish to get into trouble, was to get rid of it immediately. Delay was getting dangerous. She was standing near the back entrance of the stage when she was looking for a place to hide the picture. Beside the stage entrance there was a little room containing all the lighting switches for the stage, various battery boxes and other electrical equipment, together with a motley collection of stage properties. Quick as a flash Hinpoha opened the door of this room, darted in and hid the picture in a roll of cheesecloth. When she came out one of the teachers was standing directly before the door, pointing out to a friend the construction of the stage.

"Have we a new electrician?" he inquired genially, as he saw her coming out of the electric room. Hinpoha laughed at his pleasantry, but she was flushed and uncomfortable from the excitement of the last moment. Hinpoha was a poor dissembler. She went upstairs until the art room was empty of visitors and then returned swiftly to the electric room for the picture. She slipped it under her middy blouse, where it was safe from detection, and sped upstairs with it. As she crossed the hall to the stairs she met the same teacher the second time. "Well, you must be an electrician," he said; "that's twice you've rushed out of there in such a businesslike manner," Hinpoha laughed, but flushed painfully. It seemed to her that his eyes could look right through her middy and see the picture underneath. This time the coast was clear in the room where the pictures were and she deposited the adventurous water color safely. She heaved a great sigh of relief when she realized that the danger was over and she had nothing more to conceal. She trudged home through the snow light-heartedly, with a warm feeling that she had been the means of saving a friend from disgrace.

Sahwah, who was in the play and had a right to go up on the stage, which was all ready set for the first scene, ran in to see how things looked late in the afternoon. The school was practically empty. All the rest of the cast had gone home to get some sleep to fit them for the ordeal of the coming performance, and the teachers who had been looking at the paintings had also left. The rest of the building was in darkness, as twilight had already fallen. One set of lights was burning on the stage. Sahwah had no special business on the stage, she was simply curious to see what it looked like. Sahwah never stopped to analyze her motives for doing things. She paused to admire the statue of Joan of Arc, standing in all the majesty of its nine-foot height. This was the first chance she had had to examine it leisurely. In the rehearsal the night before she had merely seen it in a general way as she whisked off and on the stage in her part.

The construction of the thing fascinated her, and she opened the door in the skirt to satisfy her curiosity about the inner workings of the miraculous halo. She saw how the thing was done and then became interested in the inside of the statue itself. There was plenty of room in it to conceal a person. Just for the fun of the thing Sahwah got inside and drew the door shut after her, trying to imagine herself a fugitive hiding in there. There were no openings in the skirt part, but up above the waist line there were various holes to admit air. "It's no fun hiding in a statue if you can't see what's going on outside," thought Sahwah, and so she stood up straight, as in this position her eyes would come on a level with one of the holes. She could see out without being seen herself, just as if she were looking through the face piece of a suit of armor. The fun she got out of this sport, however, soon changed to dismay when she tried to get down again. It had taken some squeezing to get her head into the upper space, and now she found that she was wedged securely in. She could not move her head one particle. What was worse, a quantity of cotton wool, which had been put inside the upper part of the body for some reason or other, was dislodged by her squeezing in and pressed against her mouth, forming an effective silencer. Thus, while she could see out over the stage, she could not call out for help. Her hands were pinioned down at her sides, and by standing up she had brought her knees into a narrow place so that they were wedged together and she could not attract attention by kicking. Here was a pretty state of affairs. The benign Maid of Orleans had Sahwah in as merciless a grip as that with which the famous Iron Maiden of medieval times crushed out the lives of its victims.

Sahwah knew that her failure to come from school would call out a search, but who would ever look for her in the statue on the stage? Her only hope was to wait until the play was in progress and the door was opened to conceal the child. Then another thought startled her into a perspiration. She was in the opening scene of the play. If she was not there, the play could not commence. They would spend the evening searching for her and the statue would not be opened. What would they do about the play? The house was sold out and the people would come to see the performance and there would be none. All on account of her stupidity in wedging herself inside of the statue. Sahwah called herself severe names as she languished in her prison. Fortunately there were enough holes in the thing to supply plenty of ventilation, otherwise it might have gone hard with her. The cramped position became exceedingly tiresome. She tried, by forcing her weight against the one side or the other, to throw the statue over, thinking that it would attract attention in this way and some one would be likely to open it, but the heavy wooden base to which it was fastened held it secure. Sahwah was caught like a rat in a trap. The minutes passed like hours. Sounds died away in the building, as the last of the lingerers on the downstairs floor took themselves off through the front entrance. She could hear the slam of the heavy door and then a shout as one boy hailed another in greeting. Then silence over everything.

A quarter, or maybe a half, hour dragged by on leaden feet. Suddenly, without noise or warning, two figures appeared on the stage, coming on through the back entrance. Sahwah's heart beat joyfully. Here was some one to look over the scenery again and if she could only attract their attention they would liberate her. She made a desperate effort and wrenched her mouth open to call, only to get it full of fuzzy cotton wool that nearly choked her. There was no hope then, but that they would open the door of the statue and find her accidentally. She could hear the sound of talking in low voices. The boys were on the other side of the statue, where she could not see them.

"Let it down easy," she heard one of them say.

"Better get around on the other side," said a second voice.

The boy thus spoken to moved around until he was directly before the opening in front of Sahwah's eyes. With a start she recognized Joe Lanning. What business had Joe Lanning on the stage at this time? He was not in the play and he did not belong to the Thessalonian Society. There was only one explanation—Joe was up to some mischief again. She had not the slightest doubt that the other voice belonged to Abraham Goldstein, and thus indeed it proved, for a moment later he moved around so as to come into range of her vision. The two withdrew a few paces and looked at the statue, holding a hasty colloquy in inaudible tones, and then Joe, mounting a chair, laid hold of the Maid just above the waist line, while Abraham seized the wooden base. Sahwah felt her head going down and her feet going up. The boys were carrying the statue off the stage and out through the back entrance, over the little bridge at the back of the stage and into the hall. It was the queerest ride Sahwah had ever taken.

The boys paused before the elevator, which seemed to be standing ready with the door open. "Will she go in?" asked Abraham.

"I'm afraid not," answered Joe. "Well have to carry her downstairs." Sahwah shuddered. Would she go down head first or feet first? They carried her head first and she was dizzy with the rush of blood to her head before the two long flights were accomplished. At the foot of the last flight they laid the statue down. The hall was in total darkness.

"What are you doing?" asked the voice of Joe. Abraham was apparently producing something from somewhere. In a minute Joe was laughing. "Good stunt," he said approvingly. "Where did you get them?"

"Swiped them out of Room 22, where all the stuff for the play is." Joe flashed a small pocket electric light and by its glimmer Sahwah could see him adjusting a false beard—the one that was to be worn by the villain in the play. Abraham was apparently disguising himself in a similar fashion. This accomplished they picked up the statue again and carried it down the half flight of stairs to the back entrance of the school. For some mysterious reason this door was open. Just outside stood an automobile truck. At the back of the school lay the wide athletic field, extending for several acres. The nearest street was all of four blocks away. In the darkness it was impossible to see across this stretch of space and distinguish the actions of the two conspirators in the event people should be passing along this street. Even if the truck itself were seen that would cause no comment, for deliveries were constantly being made at the rear entrance of the school.

The statue was lifted into the truck, covered with a piece of canvas, and Joe and Abraham sprang to the driver's seat and started the machine. Sahwah very nearly suffocated under that canvas. Fortunately the ride was a short one. In about seven or eight minutes she felt the bump as they turned into a driveway, and then the truck came to a stop. The boys jumped down from the seat, opened a door which slid back with a scraping noise like a barn door and then lifted the statue from the truck and carried it into a building. From the light of their pocket flashes Sahwah could make out that she was in a barn, which was evidently unused. It was entirely empty. Setting the statue in a corner, the boys went out, closing the door after them. Sahwah was left in total darkness, and in a ten times worse position than she had been in before. On the stage at school there was some hope of the statue's being opened eventually, but here she could remain for weeks before being discovered. Sahwah began to wonder just how long she could hold out before she starved. She was hungry already.

She closed her eyes with weariness from her strained position, and it is possible that she dozed off for a few moments. In fact, that was what she did do. She dreamed that she was at the circus and all the wild animals had broken loose and were running about the audience. She could hear the roar of the lions and the screeching of the tigers. She woke up with a start and thought for a moment that her dream was true. The barn was full of wild animals which were roaring and chasing each other around. Then her senses cleared and she recognized the heavy bark of a large dog and the startled mi-ou of a cat. The dog was chasing the cat around the barn. She felt the slight thud as the cat leaped up and found refuge on top of the statue. She could hear it spitting at the dog and knew that its back was arched in an attitude of defiance. The dog barked furiously down below. Then, overcome by rage, he made a wild jump for the cat and lunged his heavy body against the side of the statue. It toppled over against the corner. For an instant Sahwah thought she was going to be killed. But the corner of the barn saved the statue from falling over altogether. It simply leaned back at a slight angle. But there was something different in her position now. At first she did not know what it was. Before this her feet were standing squarely on the wooden base of the statue, but now they were slipping around and seemed to be dangling. Then she realized what had happened. The shock of the dog's onslaught had knocked the statue clear off the base, and had also contrived to loosen her knees a little. To her joy she found that she could move her feet—could walk. For all the statue was immense, it was light, and wedged into it as she was she balanced the upper part of it perfectly. She moved out from the corner.

The dog was still barking furiously and circling around the barn after the cat. Then the cat found a paneless window by which she had entered and disappeared into the night. The dog, who had also entered by that window when chasing the cat, had been helped on the outside by a box which stood under the sill, but there was no such aid on the inside and he did not attempt to make the jump from the floor, but stood barking until the place shook. Just then a voice was heard on the outside. "Lion, Lion," it called, "where are you?" Lion barked in answer. "Come out of that barn," commanded the voice of a small boy. Lion answered again in the only way he knew how. "Wait a minute, Lion, I'm coming," said the small boy. Sahwah heard some one fumbling at the door and then it was drawn open. The light from a street lamp streamed in. It fell directly on the statue as Sahwah took another step forward. The boy saw the apparition and fled in terror, followed by the dog, leaving the door wide open. Sahwah hastened to the door. Here she encountered a difficulty. The statue was nine feet high and the door was only about eight. Naturally the statue could not bend. It had been carried in in a horizontal position. Sahwah reflected a moment. Her powers of observation were remarkably good and she could sense things that went on around her without having to see them. She had noticed that when the boys carried the statue into the barn they had had to climb up into the doorway. The inclined entrance approach had undoubtedly rotted away. She figured that this step up had been a foot at least. Her ingenious mind told her that by standing close to the edge of the doorway and jumping down she would come clear of the doorway. She put this theory to trial immediately. The scheme worked. She landed on her feet on the snow-covered ground, with the top of the statue free in the air.

As fast as she could she made her way up the driveway. Her hands were still pinioned at her sides. As she passed the house in front of the barn she could see by the street light that it was empty. A grand scheme it would have been indeed, if it had worked, hiding the statue in the unused barn where it would not have been discovered for weeks, or possibly months. Of course, Sahwah readily admitted, Joe did not know that she was in the statue; his object had merely been to spoil the play. And a very effective method he had taken, too, for the play without the statue of Joan of Arc would have been nothing.

Sahwah stood still on the street and tried to get her bearings. She was in an unfamiliar neighborhood. She walked up the street. Coming toward her was a man. Sahwah breathed a sigh of relief. Without a doubt he would see the trouble she was in and free her. Now Sahwah did not know it, but in the scramble with the dog the button had been pushed which worked the halo. The neighborhood she was in was largely inhabited by foreigners, and the man coming toward her was a Hungarian who had not been long in this country. Taking his way homeward with never a thought in his mind but his dinner, he suddenly looked up to see the gigantic figure of a woman bearing down on him, brandishing a gleaming sword and with a dim halo playing around her head. For an instant he stood rooted to the spot, and then with a wild yell he ran across the street, darted between two houses and disappeared over the back fence. Then began a series of encounters which threw Sahwah into hysterics twenty years later when she happened to remember them. Intent only on her own liberation she was at the time unconscious of the terrifying figure she presented, and hastened along at the top of her speed. Everywhere the people fled before her in the extremity of terror. On all sides she could hear shrieks of "War!" "War!" "It is a sign of war!"

In one street through which she passed lived a simple Slovak priest. He was sorely torn over the sad conflict raging in Europe and was undecided whether he should preach a sermon advocating peace at all costs or preparation for fighting. He debated the question back and forth in his mind, and, unable to come to any decision in the narrow confines of his little house, walked up and down on the cold porch seeking for light in the matter. "Oh, for a sign from heaven," he sighed, "such as came to the saints of old to solve their troublesome questions!" Scarcely had the wish passed through his mind when a vision appeared. Down the dark street came rushing the heroic image of Joan of Arc, with sword uplifted, her head shining with the refulgence of the halo. At his gate she paused and stood a long time looking at him. Sahwah thought that he would come down and help her out. Instead he fell on his knees on the porch and bowed his head, crying out something in a foreign tongue. Seeing that expectation of help from that quarter was useless, Sahwah ran on and turned a nearby corner. When the priest lifted his head again the vision was gone. "It is to be war, then," he muttered. "I have a divine command to bid my people take up arms in battle." This was the origin of the military demonstration which took place in the Slovak settlement the following Sunday, which ended in such serious rioting.

Sahwah, running onward, suddenly found herself in the very middle of the road where two carlines crossed each other. This was a very congested corner and a policeman was stationed there to direct the traffic. This policeman, however, on this cold February day, found Mike McCarty's saloon on the corner a much pleasanter place than the middle of the road, and paid one visit after another, while the traffic directed itself. This last time he had stayed inside much longer than he had intended to, having become involved in an argument with the proprietor of the place, and coming to himself with a guilty start he hurried out to resume his duties. On the sidewalk he stood as if paralyzed. In the middle of the road, in his place, stood an enormously tall woman, directing the traffic with a gleaming sword. "Mother av Hiven," he muttered superstitiously, "it's one of the saints come down to look after the job I jumped, and waiting to strike me dead when I come back." He turned on his heel and fled up the street without once looking over his shoulder.

And thus Sahwah went from place to place, vainly looking for some one who would pull her out of the statue, and leaving everywhere she went a trail of superstitious terror, such as had never been known in the annals of the city. For a week the papers were full of the mysterious appearance of the armed woman, which was taken as a presumptive augury of war. Many affirmed that she had stopped them on the street and commanded them in tones of thunder to take up arms to save the country from destruction, and promising to lead them to victory when the time for battle came. Many of the foreigners believed to their dying day that they had seen a vision from heaven. Sahwah at last got her bearings and found that she was not a great distance from the school, so she took her way thither where she might encounter some one who was connected with the play and knew of the existence of the statue, a secret which was being closely guarded from the public, that the effect might be greater.

She nearly wept with joy when she saw Dick Albright just about to enter the building. Although he was startled almost out of a year's growth at the sight of the statue, which he supposed to be standing on the stage in the building, running up the front steps after him, he did not disappear into space as had all of the others she had met. After the first fright he suspected some practical joke and stood still to see what would happen next. Sahwah knew that the only thing visible of her was her feet and that she could not explain matters with her voice, so, coming close to Dick, she stretched out her foot as far as possible. Now Sahwah, with her riotous love of color, had bright red buttons on her black shoes, the only set like them in the school. Dick recognized the buttons and knew that it was Sahwah in the statue. He still thought she was playing a joke, and laughed uproariously. Sahwah grew desperate. She must make him understand that she wanted him to pull her out. The broad stone terrace before the door was covered with a light fall of snow. With the point of her toe she traced in the snow the words

"PULL ME OUT."

Dick now took in the situation. He opened the door of the statue and with some difficulty succeeded in extricating Sahwah from her precarious position. Together they carried the much-traveled Maid into the building and up the stairs and set her in place on the stage. She had just been missed by the arriving players and the place was in an uproar. Sahwah told what had happened that afternoon and the adventures she had had in getting back to the school, while her listeners exclaimed incredulously. There was no longer time to go home for supper so Sahwah ran off to the green room to begin making up for her part in the play.

CHAPTER X.

WHO CUT THE WIRE?

The house was packed on this the first night of the Thessalonian play. It was already long past time for the performance to begin. The orchestra finished the overture and waited a few minutes; then began another selection. They played this through, and there was still no indication of the curtain going up. They played a third piece. The house became restless and began to clap for the appearance of the performers. No sign from the stage. Behind the curtain there was pandemonium. When everything was about ready to begin it was discovered that none of the stage lights would work. Neither the foot lights nor the big cluster up over the center of the stage nor any of the side lights could be turned on. A hasty examination of the wiring led to the discovery that the wires which supplied the current had been cut in the room where the switchboard was. The plaster had been broken into in order to reach them. This was the reason that the play was not beginning. The President of the Thessalonians came out in front and explained to the audience that something had gone wrong with the lights, which would cause a delay in the rising of the curtain, but the trouble was being fixed and he begged the indulgence of the house for a few minutes. The orchestra filled in the time by playing lively marches, while the boys behind the scenes worked feverishly to mend the severed wires, and the curtain went up a whole hour after scheduled time.

The first act went off famously. Gladys was a born actress and sustained the difficult role of Marie Latour well. The part where she defies her tyrannical father brought down the house. Sahwah came in for her share of applause too. Seeing her composed manner and hearing her calm voice, no one in the audience could ever have guessed the strenuous experience she had just been through. In the second scene Marie, driven from her home, wanders around in the streets with her child, until, faint from hunger, she sinks to the ground. The scene is laid before the wall of her father's large estate and she falls at his very gates. Gladys made the scene very realistic, and the audience sat tense and sympathetic. "Food, food," moaned Marie Latour, "only a crust to keep the life in me and my child!" She lay weakly in the road, unable to rise. "Food, food," she moaned again. At this moment there suddenly descended, as from the very heavens, a ham sandwich on the end of a string. It dangled within an inch of her nose. Gladys was petrified. The audience sat up in surprise, and a ripple of laughter ran through the house. It was such an unexpected anticlimax. That some one was playing a practical joke Gladys did not for a moment doubt, and she was furious at this ridiculous interruption of her big scene. In the play Marie loses consciousness and is found by a peasant, and it is on this occurrence that the rest of the play hinges. The sudden appearance of the ham sandwich in response to her cry for food was fatal to the pathos of the scene. The rest of the cast, standing in the wings, saw what had happened and were at their wits' end. But Gladys was equal to the occasion.

Moving her head wearily and passing her hand over her eyes she murmured faintly but audibly, "Cruel, cruel mirage to taunt me thus! Vanish, thou image of a fevered brain, thou absurd memory! Come not to mock me!" The actors in the wings, taking their cue from her speech, found the string to which the sandwich was tied and jerked it. The sandwich vanished from the sight of the audience. The scene was saved. The spectators simply passed it over as a more or less clumsy attempt to portray a vision of a disordered brain. The string on the sandwich had been passed over certain rigging above the stage that moved the scenery, and on through a little ventilator that came out on the fourth floor, from which point the manipulator had been able to listen to the speeches on the stage and time the drop of the sandwich. By the time the Thessalonian boys had traced the string to its end the perpetrator of the joke was nowhere to be found. He had fled as soon as the thing had been lowered. The scene ended without further calamity.

In the third scene—the one in the peasant's hut—there is a cat on the stage. The presence of this cat was the signal for further trouble. In one of the tense passages, where Marie Latour is pleading with the son of the peasant to flee for his life before the agents of her father come and capture them both, and the cat lies asleep on the hearth, there was a sudden uproar, and a dog bounded through the entrance of the stage. The cat rushed around in terror and finally ran up the curtain. The lovers parted hastily and tried to capture the dog, but eluding their pursuit he jumped over the footlights into the orchestra, landing with a crash on the keys of the piano, and then out into the audience. Nyoda and three or four of the Winnebagos, sitting together near the front on the first floor of the auditorium, recognized the dog with a good deal of surprise. It was Mr. Bob, Hinpoha's black cocker spaniel. How he had gotten in was a mystery, for Hinpoha herself was not there. Nyoda called to him sharply and he came to her wagging his tail, and allowed himself to be put out with the best nature in the world. But the scene had been spoiled.

During the rest of the evening Nyoda, as well as a number of the other teachers, sat with brows knitted, going over the various things that had happened to interrupt that play. As yet they did not know about the attempt to steal the statue, which Sahwah had accidentally nipped in the bud. But the following week, when the play was all over, and the various occurrences had been made known, there was a day of reckoning at Washington High School. Joe Lanning and Abraham Goldstein were called up before the principal and confronted with Sahwah, who told, to their infinite amazement, every move they had made in carrying off the statue. At first they denied everything as a made-up story gotten up to spite them, but when Sahwah led the way to the barn where she had been confined and triumphantly produced the base of the statue, they saw that further denial was useless and admitted their guilt. They also confessed to being the authors of the sandwich joke and the ones who had brought in the dog. Both were expelled from school.

But the thing which the principal and teachers considered the bigger crime—the cutting of the wires at the back of the stage—was still a mystery. Joe's and Abraham's complicity in the statue affair furnished them with a complete alibi in regard to the other. It was proven, beyond a doubt, that they had not been in the building in the early part of the afternoon nor after they had carried off the statue, until after the wires had been cut. Then who had cut the wires? That was the question that agitated the school. It was too big a piece of vandalism to let slip. The principal, Mr. Jackson, was determined to run down the offender. Joe and Abraham denied all knowledge of the affair and there was no clue. The whole school was up in arms about the matter.

Then things took a rather unexpected turn. In one of the teachers' meetings where the matter was being discussed, one of the teachers, Mr. Wardwell, suddenly got to his feet. He had just recollected something. "I remember," he said, "seeing Dorothy Bradford coming out of the electric room late on the afternoon of the play. She came out twice, once about three o'clock and once about four. Each time she seemed embarrassed about meeting me and turned scarlet." There was a murmur of surprise among the teachers. Nyoda sat up very straight.

The next day Hinpoha was summoned to the office. Unsuspectingly she went. She had been summoned before, always on matters of more or less congenial business. She found Mr. Jackson, Mr. Wardwell and Nyoda together in the private office.

"Miss Bradford," began Mr. Jackson, without preliminary, "Mr. Wardwell tells me he saw you coming out of the electric room on the afternoon of the play. In view of what happened that night, the presence of anybody in that room looks suspicious. Will you kindly state what you did in there?"

Nyoda listened with an untroubled heart, sure of an innocent and convincing reason why Hinpoha had been in that room. Hinpoha, taken completely by surprise, was speechless. To Nyoda's astonishment and dismay, she turned fiery red. Hinpoha always blushed at the slightest provocation. In the stress of the moment she could not think of a single worth-while excuse for having gone into the electric room. Telling the real reason was of course out of the question because she had promised to shield Emily Meeks.

"I left something in there," she stammered, "and went back after it."

"You carried nothing in your hands either time when you came out," said

Mr. Wardwell.

Hinpoha was struck dumb. She was a poor hand at deception and was totally unable to "bluff" anything through. "I didn't say I carried anything out," she said in an agitated voice. "I went in after something and it—wasn't there."

"What was it?" asked Mr. Jackson.

"I can't tell you," said Hinpoha.

"How did you happen to leave anything in the electric room?" persisted

Mr. Jackson. "What were you doing in there in the first place?"

"I went in to see if I had left something there," said poor Hinpoha, floundering desperately in the attempt to tell a plausible tale and yet not lie deliberately. Then, realizing that she was contradicting herself and getting more involved all the time, she gave it up in despair and sat silent and miserable. Nyoda's expression of amazement and concern was an added torture.

"You admit, then, that you were in the electric room twice on Thursday afternoon, doing something which you cannot explain?" said Mr. Jackson, slowly. Hinpoha nodded, mutely. She never for an instant wavered in her loyalty to Emily.

"There is another thing," continued Mr. Jackson, "that seems to point to the fact that you were in league with those who wished to spoil the play. It was your dog that was let out on the stage in pursuit of the cat."

"I know it was," said Hinpoha, feeling that she was being drawn helplessly into a net from which there was no escape. "But that wasn't my fault. I haven't the slightest idea how he got there. It was pure chance that he was coaxed into the building."

"That may all be," said Mr. Jackson, with frowning wrinkles around the corners of his eyes, "but it looks suspicious."

"You certainly don't think I cut those wires, do you?" said Hinpoha incredulously.

Mr. Jackson looked wise. "You were not at the play yourself, were you?" he asked.

"No," answered Hinpoha.

"Why weren't you?" pursued Mr. Jackson. "Have you anything against the

Thessalonian Society?"

"No, not at all," said Hinpoha with a catch in her voice. "I am not going to anything this winter." She looked down at her black dress expressively, not trusting her voice to speak.

"Further," continued Mr. Jackson, "you were seen in the company of Joe Lanning the day before these things happened." Now, Hinpoha had walked home from school with Joe that Wednesday. She had done it merely because she was too courteous to snub him flatly when he had caught up with her on the street. She despised him just as the rest of the class did and avoided him whenever she could, but when brought face to face with him she had not the hardihood to refuse his company. That this innocent act should be misconstrued into meaning that she was mixed up in his doings seemed monstrous. Yet Mr. Jackson apparently believed this to be the truth. Things seemed to be closing around her. To Mr. Jackson her guilt was perfectly clear. She was a friend of Joe Lanning's; she had lent him her dog to work mischief on the stage; she admitted being in the electric room and refused to tell what she had been doing there.

"Well," he said crisply, "somebody cut those wires Thursday Afternoon, and only one person was seen going in and out of the electric room during that time, and that person is yourself. You admit that you were in there doing something which will not bear explanation. It looks pretty suspicious, doesn't it?"

"I didn't do it," Hinpoha declared stoutly.

In her distress she did not dare meet Nyoda's eyes. What was Nyoda thinking of her, anyhow?

"And so," continued Mr. Jackson, not heeding her denial, "until you can give a satisfactory explanation of your presence in the electric room last Thursday I must consider that you had something to do with the cutting of those wires. I have been asked by the Board of Education to look into the matter thoroughly and to punish the culprit with expulsion from school. As all evidence points to you as the guilty person, I shall be obliged, under the circumstances, to expel you."

Hinpoha sat as if turned to stone. The wild beating of her heart almost suffocated her. Expelled from school! But even with that terrible sentence ringing in her ears it never entered her head to betray Emily. If this was to be the price of loyalty, then she would pay the price. There was no other way. She had not been clever enough to explain her presence in the electric room to the satisfaction of Mr. Jackson and yet breathe no word of the real situation, and this was the result. Her head whirled from the sudden calamity which had overwhelmed her; her thoughts were chaos. She hardly heard when Mr. Jackson said curtly, "You may go." As one in a dream she walked out of the office. Nyoda came out with her.

"Of all things," said Mr. Wardwell to Mr. Jackson, when they were left alone, "to think that a girl should have done that thing."

"It seems strange, too," mused Mr. Jackson, "that she should have been able to do it. You would hardly look for a girl to be cutting electric wires, would you? It takes some skill to do that. Where did she learn how to do it?"

"Those Camp Fire Girls," said Mr. Wardwell emphatically, "know everything. I don't know where they learn it, but they do."

Nyoda led Hinpoha into one of the empty club rooms and sat down beside her. "Now, my dear," she said quietly, "will you please tell me the whole story? It is absurd of course to accuse you of cutting those wires, but what were you doing in that room? All you have to do is give a satisfactory explanation and the accusation will be withdrawn." Nyoda's voice was friendly and sympathetic and it was a sore temptation to Hinpoha to tell her the whole thing just as it happened. But she had promised Emily not to tell a living soul, and a promise was a promise with Hinpoha.

"Nyoda," she said steadily, "I was in that electric room twice on

Thursday afternoon. I carried something in and I carried it out again.

But I can't tell you what it was."

"Not even to save yourself from being expelled?" asked Nyoda curiously.

"Not even to save myself from being expelled," said Hinpoha steadfastly.

And Nyoda, baffled, gave it up. But of one thing she was sure. Whatever silly thing Hinpoha had done that she was ashamed to confess, she had never in the world cut those wires. It was simply impossible for her to have done such a thing. Entirely convinced on this point, Nyoda went back to Mr. Jackson, and told him her belief, begging him not to put his threat of expulsion into execution. But Mr. Jackson was obdurate. There was something under the surface of which Nyoda knew nothing. All the year there had been a certain lawless element in the school which was continually breaking out in open defiance of law and order. Mr. Jackson had been totally unable to cope with the situation. He had been severely criticised for not having succeeded in stamping out this disorder, and was accused of not being able to control his scholars. The events connected with the giving of the play had been widely published—it was impossible to keep them a secret—and Mr. Jackson had been taken to task by those above him in the educational department for not being able to find out who had cut the wires. Smarting under this censure, he had determined to fix the blame at an early date at all costs, and when the opportunity came of fastening a suspicion onto Hinpoha he had seized it eagerly, and intended to publish far and wide that he had found the guilty one. Therefore he met Nyoda's appeal with stony indifference.

"I shall consider her guilty until she has proven her innocence," he maintained obstinately, "and you will find that I am right. That is nothing but a made-up story about going in there for something she had left. You noticed how she contradicted herself half a dozen times in as many minutes. She is the guilty one, all right," and in sore distress Nyoda left him.

The axe fell and Hinpoha was expelled from school. If lightning had fallen on a clear day and cleft the roof open, the pupils could not have been more dumbfounded. Hinpoha was the very last one any one would have suspected of cutting wires. In fact, many were openly incredulous. But Mr. Jackson took care to make all the damaging facts public, and Hinpoha's fair name was dragged in the mud. Emily Meeks was one who stood loyal to Hinpoha. She was ignorant that it was to shield her Hinpoha had refused to tell what she was doing in the electric room, as she had gone home before Hinpoha had retouched the picture, but she refused to believe that her angel, as she always thought of Hinpoha, could be guilty of any wrong doing.

As for Hinpoha herself, life was not worth living. The scene with Aunt Phoebe, when she heard of her disgrace, was too painful to record here. Suffice to say that Hinpoha was regarded as a criminal of the worst type and was never allowed to forget for one instant that she had disgraced the name of Bradford forever. It was awful not to be going to school and getting lessons. Those days at home were nightmares that she remembered to the end of her life with a shudder. The only ray of comfort she had was the fact that Nyoda and the Winnebagos stood by her stanchly. "I can bear it," she said to Nyoda forlornly, "knowing that you believe in me, but if you ever went back on me I couldn't live." Nyoda urged her no more to tell her secret, for she suspected that it concerned some one else whom Hinpoha would not expose, and trusted to time to solve the mystery and remove the stain from Hinpoha's name.

The excitement over, school settled down into its old rut. Joe Lanning's father sent him away to military school and Abraham's father began to use his influence to have him reinstated. Mr. Goldstein put forth such a touching plea about Abraham's having been led astray by Joe Lanning and being no more than a tool in his hands, and Abraham promised so faithfully that he would never deviate from the path of virtue again, now that his evil genius was removed, if they would only let him come back and graduate, that he was given the chance. Nothing new came up about the cutting of the wires except that the end of a knife blade was found on the floor under the place where the hole had been made in the wall. There were no marks of identification on it and nothing was done about it.

One day, Dick Albright, in the Physics room on the third floor of the building, stood by the window and looked across at a friend of his who was standing at the window of the Chemistry room. The two rooms faced each other across an open space in the back of the building, which was designed to let more light into certain rooms. This space was only open at the third and fourth floors. The second floor was roofed over with a skylight at this point. It was after school hours and Dick was alone in the room. So, apparently, was his friend. Dick raised the window and called across the space to the other boy, who raised his window and answered him. From talking back and forth they passed to throwing a ball of twine to each other. Once Dick failed to catch it, and falling short of the window, it rolled down upon the roof of the second story.

Dick promptly climbed out of the window, and sliding down the waterspout, reached the roof and went in pursuit of the ball. One of the windows opening from the third story onto this open space was that in the electric room, and it was under this window that the ball came to a standstill. As Dick stooped to pick it up he found a knife lying beside it. He brought it along with him and climbed back into his room. Then he pulled it out and looked at it. It was an ordinary pocket knife with a horn handle. On one side of the handle there was a plate bearing the name F. Boyd. "Frank Boyd's knife," said Dick to himself. "He must have dropped it out of the window." Idly he opened the blade. It was broken off about half an inch from the point. Dick began to turn things over in his mind. A piece of a knife blade had been found in the electric room. A knife with a broken blade had been found on the roof under the window of the electric room. That knife belonged to Frank Boyd. The inference was very simple. Frank had climbed in the window of the electric room from the roof of the second story and cut the wires, and then climbed out again, and so was not seen coming out of the room into the hall. In climbing out he had dropped the knife without noticing it. He had already left a piece of the blade inside. Frank Boyd was one of the lawless spirits who had caused much of the trouble all through the year. He had also been blackballed at the last election of the Thessalonian Society. It was very easy to believe that he would try to do something to spite the Thessalonians.

Dick hastened down to Mr. Jackson's office with the knife and asked him to fit the broken piece to the shortened blade. It fitted perfectly. Beyond a doubt it was Frank Boyd and not Hinpoha who had cut the wires in the electric room. The next morning Frank was confronted with the evidence of the knife and confessed his guilt. He had been in league with Joe Lanning, and cutting the wires had been his part of the job. He had done it in the early part of the evening while the actors were making up for their parts, getting in and out of the window, just as Dick had figured out. No one had detected him in the act and the lucky incident of Hinpoha's having been seen coming out of the electric room turned all suspicion away from him. Justice in his case was tardy but certain, and Frank Boyd was expelled, and Hinpoha was reinstated. Mr. Jackson, in his elation over having caught the real culprit and effectually breaking up the "Rowdy Ring," was gracious enough to make a public apology to Hinpoha. So the blot was wiped off her scutcheon, and Emily's secret was still intact, for no one ever asked again what Hinpoha had been doing in the electric room on the afternoon of the Thessalonian play.

CHAPTER XI.

ANOTHER COASTING PARTY.

"This is the terrible Hunger Moon, the lean gray wolf can hardly bay," quoted Hinpoha, as she threw out a handful of crumbs for the birds. The ground was covered with ice and snow, and the wintry winds whistled through the bare trees in the yard, ruffling up the feathers of the poor little sparrows huddling on the branches.

Gladys stood beside Hinpoha, watching the hungry little winter citizens flying hastily down to their feast. "What is Mr. Bob barking at?" she asked, pausing to listen.

"I'll go and find out," said Hinpoha. From the porch she could see Mr. Bob standing under an evergreen tree in the back yard, barking up at it with all his might. Hinpoha came out to see what was the matter. "Hush, Mr. Bob," she commanded, throwing a snowball at him. She picked her way through the deep snow to the tree. "Oh, Gladys, come here," she called. Gladys came out and joined her.

"What is it?" she asked. Huddled up in the low branches of the tree was a great ghostly looking bird, white as the snow under their feet. Its eyes were closed and it was apparently asleep. Hinpoha stretched out her hand and touched its feathers. It woke up with a start and looked at her with great round eyes full of alarm.

"It's an owl!" said Hinpoha in amazement, "a snowy owl! It must have flown across the lake from Canada. They do sometimes when the food is scarce and the cold too intense up there." The owl blinked and closed his eyes again. The glare of the sun on the snow blinded him. He acted stupid and half frozen, and sat crouched close against the trunk of the tree, making no effort to fly away.

"How tame he is!" said Gladys. "He doesn't seem to mind us in the least." Hinpoha tried to stroke him but he jerked away and tumbled to the ground. One wing was apparently broken. Mr. Bob made a leap for the bird as he fell, but Hinpoha seized him by the collar and dragged him into the house. When she returned the owl was making desperate efforts to get up into the tree again by jumping, but without success. Hinpoha caught him easily in spite of his struggles and bore him into the house. There was an empty cage down in the cellar which had once housed a parrot, and into this the solemn-eyed creature was put.

"That wing will heal again, and then we can let him go," said Hinpoha.

"Hadn't it better be tied down?" suggested Gladys. "He flutters it so much." With infinite pains Hinpoha tied the broken wing down to the bird's side, using strips of gauze bandage for the purpose. The owl made no sound. They fixed a perch in the cage and he stepped decorously up on it and regarded them with an intense, mournful gaze. "Isn't he spooky looking?" said Gladys, shivering and turning away. "He gives me the creeps."

"What will we feed him?" asked Hinpoha.

"Do owls eat crumbs?" asked Gladys.

Hinpoha shook her head. "That isn't enough. I've always read that they catch mice and things like that to eat." She brightened up. "There are several mice in the trap now. I saw them when I brought up the cage." She sped down cellar and returned with three mice in a trap.

"Ugh," said Gladys in disgust, as Hinpoha pulled them out by the tails.

She put them in the cage with the owl and he pecked at them hungrily.

"What will your aunt say when she sees him?" asked Gladys.

"I don't know," said Hinpoha doubtfully. Aunt Phoebe was away for the afternoon and so had not been in a position to interfere thus far.

"Maybe I had better take the cage home with me," suggested Gladys.

"No," said Hinpoha firmly, "I want him myself. I'll tell you what I'll do. I'll put the cage up in the attic and she'll never know I have him. I can slip up and feed him. It would be better for him up there, anyway. It's too warm for him downstairs. He's used to a cold climate." So "Snowy," as they had christened him, was established by a window under the eaves on the third floor, where he could look out at the trees for which he would be pining. Aunt Phoebe always took a nap after lunch, and this gave Hinpoha a chance to run up and look at her patient. She fed him on chicken feed and mice when there were any. Never did he show the slightest sign of friendliness or recognition when she hovered over him; but continued to stare sorrowfully at her with an unblinking eye. If he liked his new lodging under the cozy eaves he made no mention of it, and if he pined for his winter palace in the Canadian forest he was equally uncommunicative. Hinpoha longed to poke him in order to make him give some expression of feeling. But at all events, he did not struggle against his captivity, and Hinpoha reflected judicially that after all it was a good thing that he had such a stolid personality, for a calm frame of mind aids the recovery of the patient and he would not be likely to keep his wing from healing by dashing it against the side of the cage. It seemed almost as though he knew his presence in the house was a secret, and was in league with Hinpoha not to betray himself. So Aunt Phoebe lived downstairs in blissful ignorance of the feathered boarder in the attic.

She was suffering from a cold that week and was more than usually exacting. She finally took to her bed in an air-tight room with a mustard plaster and an electric heating pad, expressing her intention of staying there until her cold was cured. "But you ought to have some fresh air," protested Hinpoha, "you'll smother in there with all that heat."

"You leave that window shut," said Aunt Phoebe crossly. "All this foolishness about open windows makes me tired. It's a pity if a young girl has to tell her elders what's best for them. Now bring the History of the Presbyterian Church, and read that seventh chapter over again; my mind was preoccupied last night and I did not hear it distinctly." This was Aunt Phoebe's excuse for having fallen asleep during the reading. So poor Hinpoha had to sit in that stifling room and read until she thought she would faint. Aunt Phoebe fell asleep presently, however, to her great relief, and she stole out softly, leaving the door open behind her so that some air could get in from the hall.

Aunt Phoebe woke up in the middle of the night feeling decidedly uncomfortable. She was nearly baked with the heat that was being applied on all sides. She turned off the heating pad and threw back one of the covers, and as she grew more comfortable sleep began to hover near. She was just sinking off into a doze when she suddenly started up in terror. There was a presence in the room—something white was moving silently toward the bed. Aunt Phoebe was terribly superstitious and believed in ghosts as firmly as she believed in the gospel. She always expected to see a sheeted figure standing in the hall some night, its hand outstretched in solemn warning. But this ghost was more terrifying than any she had ever imagined. It was not in the form of a being at all—just a formless Thing that moved with strange jerks and starts, sometimes rising at least a foot in the air. The hair stood up straight on Aunt Phoebe's head, and her lips became so dry they cracked. Then her heart almost stopped beating altogether. The ghost rose in the air and stood on her bed, where it continued its uncanny movements. Aunt Phoebe folded her hands and began to pray. The ghost sailed upward once more and stood on the foot board of her bed. Aunt Phoebe prayed harder. "Hoot!" said the ghost. Aunt Phoebe moaned. "Hoot!" said the ghost. Aunt Phoebe tried to scream, but her throat was paralyzed. "Hoot!" said the ghost. Aunt Phoebe found her voice. "WOW-OW-OW-OW!" she screeched in tones that could have been heard a block.

Hinpoha jumped clear out of bed in one leap and reached Aunt Phoebe's room in one more. Visions of burglars and fire were in her mind. Hastily she turned on the light. Aunt Phoebe was sitting up in bed still screaming at the top of her lungs, and on the footboard of the bed sat Snowy, blinking in the sudden light. Hinpoha stood frozen to the spot. How had the bird gotten out? "Snowy!" she stammered. The owl looked at her with his old solemn stare, and then slowly he winked one eye. "Stop screaming, Aunt Phoebe," said Hinpoha; "it's nothing but an owl."

"An owl!" exclaimed Aunt Phoebe faintly. "How could an owl get in here with all the doors and windows shut?"

"But I left your door open when I went out," said Hinpoha, "and Snowy must have gotten out of his cage and come down the attic stairs."

"Must have gotten out of his cage!" echoed Aunt Phoebe. "Do you mean to tell me that you have an owl in a cage somewhere in this house?" There was no use denying the fact any more, as Snowy had given himself away so completely, and Hinpoha told about finding the snowy owl in the yard and putting it up in the cage. "What next!" gasped Aunt Phoebe. "I suppose I shall wake up some morning and find a boa constrictor in my bed."

"I'm sorry he frightened you so," said Hinpoha contritely, "but I'll see that he doesn't get out again. I may keep him until his wing heals, mayn't I?" she asked pleadingly.

"I suppose there's no getting around you," sighed Aunt Phoebe, sinking back on her pillow. "If it wasn't a bird you'd be having something else. Only keep him out of my sight!" Hinpoha caught the owl and carried him out with many flutters and pecks. The cage door stood open and the wires were bent out, showing where his powerful bill had pecked until he gained his freedom. Hinpoha fastened him in again and he stepped decorously up on his perch and sat there in such a dignified attitude that it was hard to believe him capable of breaking jail and entering a lady's bedroom.

Aunt Phoebe spent the next day in bed, recovering from her fright. This was the night of the Camp Fire meeting which Hinpoha had been given permission to attend. She had been in such a fever of anticipation all week that Aunt Phoebe was surprised when she came into her room after supper and sat down with the History of the Presbyterian Church. "Well, aren't you going to that precious meeting of yours?" she asked sharply.

"I think," said Hinpoha slowly, "that I had better stay at home with you."

"I won't die without you," said Aunt Phoebe drily. "I can ring for Mary if I want anything."

A mighty struggle was going on inside of Hinpoha. First she saw in her mind's eye her beloved Winnebagos, having a meeting at Nyoda's house, the place where she best loved to go to meetings, waiting to welcome her back into their midst with open arms; and then she saw this cross old woman, her aunt, sick and lonesome, left alone in the house with a maid who despised her. With the cup of enjoyment raised to her lips she set it down again. "I think I would rather stay with you, Aunt Phoebe," she said simply. And in the Desert of Waiting there blossomed a fragrant rose!

The deferred celebration for Hinpoha's return into the Winnebago fold was held the following week. With the joy of the returned pilgrim she took her place in the Council Circle, and once more joined in singing, "Burn, Fire, Burn," and "Mystic Fire," and this time when Nyoda called the roll and pronounced the name "Hinpoha," she was answered by a joyous "Kolah" instead of the sorrowful silence which had followed that name for so many weeks.

February froze, thawed, snowed and sleeted itself off the calendar, and March set in like a roaring lion, with a worse snowstorm than even the Snow Moon had produced. Venturesome treebuds, who loved the warm sun like Aunt Phoebe loved her heating pad, and who had crept out of their dark blankets one balmy day in February to be nearer the genial heat giver, shivered until their sap froze in their veins, and a drab-colored phoebe bird, who had nested under the eaves of the Bradford porch the year before, coming back to his summer residence according to the date marked on his calendar, huddled disconsolately beside the old nest, feeling sure that he would contract bronchitis before the wife of his bosom arrived to join him.

Hinpoha listened to his disgruntled "pewit phoebe, pewit phoebe," and made haste to throw him some crumbs. It seemed like a delicious joke to her that he should be calling so plaintively for his phoebe, not knowing that there was a Phoebe on the premises all the while. And one day the little mate came and both birds forgot the snow and cold in the joy of their reunion. Phoebes consider it extremely indecorous to travel in mixed company, (just like Aunt Phoebe, thought Hinpoha humorously,) so the females linger behind for several days after the males start north and join them in the seclusion of their own homes. Hinpoha's heart sang in sympathy with the joy of the reunited lovers.

Sahwah had come over to get her lessons with Hinpoha, and as she turned the leaves of her "Cicero" a little red heart dropped out on the floor.

Hinpoha stooped to pick it up. "What's this?" she asked with interest.

Sahwah blushed.

"Ned Roberts—you remember Ned Roberts up at camp—sent it to me for a valentine." Hinpoha went back in her thoughts to the dance at the Mountain Lake Camp the summer before, where she had had such a royal good time. How far removed that time seemed now!

"I wonder if Sherry ever writes to Nyoda," she said musingly.

"I don't believe he does," said Sahwah, "for Nyoda has never said anything." If they could have seen Nyoda at that very moment, reading a certain letter and thrusting it into her bureau drawer with a pile of others bearing the same post-mark, they would really have had something to gossip about.

"Did you ever see such a snowfall in March?" said Hinpoha, looking out the window at the white landscape.

"It must be perfectly grand coasting," said Sahwah, ever with an eye for sport. "Dick Albright promised he would take us out on his new bob the next time there was snow, and this is the next time, and will probably be the last time. Do you suppose you could come along?"

"I doubt it," said Hinpoha. "Aunt Phoebe thinks coasting is too rough. Did I ever tell you the time mother and I coasted down the walk and ran into Aunt Phoebe?" Sahwah laughed heartily over the story.

"Poor Aunt Phoebe!" she said, wiping the tears of laughter from her eyes. "She is bound to get all the shocks that flesh is heir to."

As she was walking home through the snow that afternoon some one came up behind her and took her books from her hand. It was Dick Albright. "Good afternoon, Miss Brewster," he said formally.

"Good afternoon, Mr. Albright," said Sahwah in the same tone, her eyes dancing in her head. Then she burst out, "Oh, Dick, won't you take us coasting to-morrow night? This is positively the last snow of the season."

"Sure," said Dick. "Take you to-night if you want to."

Sahwah shook her head. "'Strictly nothing doing,' to quote your own elegant phrase," she said. "I've a German test on to-morrow morning, and consequently have an engagement with my friend Wilhelm Tell to-night. I've simply got to get above eighty-five in this test or go below passing for the month. I got through last month without ever looking at it, but it won't work again this month."

"How did you do it?" asked Dick.

"Why," answered Sahwah, "when it came to the test and we were asked to tell the story of the book I simply wrote down, 'I can't tell you that one, but I can tell another just as good,' and I did. Old Prof. Frühlingslied was so floored by my 'blooming cheek' that he passed me, but he has had a watchful eye on me ever since." Dick laughed outright.

"I never saw anything like you," he said, swinging her books around in his hand. The red heart fell out into the snow. Dick picked it up. "Who's your friend?" he said, deliberately reading the name, and immediately filled with jealous pangs. Dick liked Sahwah better than any girl in school. Her irrepressible, fun—loving nature held him fascinated. Sahwah liked Dick, too, but no better than she liked most of the boys in the class. Sahwah was a poor hand to regard a boy as a "beau." Boys were good things to skate with, or play ball or go rowing with; they came in handy when there were heavy things to lift, and all that; but in none of these things did one seem to have any advantage over the others, so it was immaterial to her which one she had a good time with. The good time was the main thing to her. Sahwah had a fifteen—year—old brother, and she knew what a boy was under his white collar and "boiled" shirt. There was no silly sentimentality in her spicy make-up. She was a royal good companion when there was any fun going on, but it was about as easy to "get soft" with her as with a stone fence post. She was a master hand at ridicule and the boys knew this and respected her accordingly. In spite of all this Dick's admiration of her remained steadfast, and he would have attempted to jump over the moon if she had dared him to do it. Hence the valentine signed "Ned Roberts" piqued him. Sahwah had ordered him not to send her one and he had meekly obeyed. It hurt him to think any one else had the right to do it.

"Who's your friend?" he repeated as he handed her the heart.

"Oh, somebody," said Sahwah, enjoying the opportunity of teasing him. And that was all he could get out of her, in spite of numerous questions.

"You'll surely go coasting to-morrow night?" he said as he left her in front of her house.

"I surely will,"' said Sahwah, flashing him a brilliant smile, "I wouldn't miss it for the world!" If ever a girl had the power to allure and torment a boy that girl was Sahwah.

* * * * *

The house belonging to the Gardiners was now rented, together with the furnished room, and brought in thirty dollars a month, which made housekeeping much smoother sailing for Migwan, but the fact still remained that the money which was to have put her into college the next year was spent, and there was no present prospect of replacing it. Her mother was now home from the hospital and fully on the road to recovery, and Migwan tried to make her happiness over this fact overbalance her disappointment at her own loss. None of her stories or picture plays had been accepted, and of late she had had to give up writing, for with her mother sick most of the housework fell on her shoulders. Although she maintained a bright and cheery exterior, she went about mourning in secret for her lost career, as she called it, and the heart went out of her studying.

She was walking soberly through the hall at school one morning when she heard somebody call out, "Oh, Miss Gardiner, come here a minute." It was Professor Green, standing in the door of his class room. "There is something I want to tell you about," he said, smiling down at her when she came up to him. "You like to study History pretty well, don't you?" Migwan nodded. Next to Latin, history was her favorite study. "Well," resumed Professor Green, "here is a chance for you to do something with it. You remember that Professor Parsons who lectured to the school on various historical subjects last winter? You know he is a perfect crank on having boys and girls learn history. He has now offered a prize of $100 to the boy or girl in the graduating class of this High School who can pass the best examination in Ancient, Medieval and Modern History. You have had all three of those subjects, have you not?"

"Yes," said Migwan, eagerly.

"The examination is to take place the last week in April," continued Professor Green. "'A word to the wise is sufficient.' You are one of the best students of history in the class."

Migwan went away after thanking him for telling her about it, feeling as if she were treading on air. There was no doubt in her mind about her ability to learn history, as there was about geometry. She had an amazing memory for dates and events and in her imaginative mind the happenings of centuries ago took form and color and stood out as vividly as if she saw them passing by in review. Her heart beat violently when she thought that she had as good a chance, if not better than any one else in the class, of winning that $100 prize. This would pay her tuition in the local university for the first year. She resolved to throw her fruitless writing to the winds and put all her strength into her history. The world stretched out before her a blooming, sunny meadow, instead of a stagnant fen, and exultantly she sang to herself one of the pageant songs of the Camp Fire Girls:

"Darkness behind us,

Peace around us,

Joy before us,

White Flame forever!"

That morning the announcement of the prize examination was made to the whole class, and Abraham Goldstein also resolved that he would win that $100.

The snow lasted over another day and the next night Sahwah and Dick Albright and a half dozen other girls and boys went coasting. It was bright moonlight and the air was clear and crisp, just cold enough to keep the snow hard and not cold enough to chill them as they sat on the bob. The place where they went coasting was down the long lake drive in the park, an unbroken stretch of over half a mile. Halfway down the slope the land rose up in a "thank—you—marm," and when the bob struck this it shot into the air and came down again in the path with a thrilling leap which never failed to make the girls shriek. Migwan was there in the crowd, and Gladys, and one or two more of the Winnebagos. Dick Albright was in his element as he steered the bob down the long white lane, for Sahwah sat right behind him, shouting merry nonsense into his ear. "Now let me steer," she commanded, when they had gone down a couple of times.

"Don't you do it, Dick," said one of the other boys, "she'll never steer us around the bend." Dick hesitated. There was a sharp turn in the road, right near the bottom of the descent, and as the bob had acquired a high degree of speed by the time it reached this point, it required quick work to make the turn.

"If you don't let me steer just once I'll never speak to you again, Dick Albright," said Sahwah, with flashing eyes. Dick wavered. The chances were that Sahwah would land them safely at the bottom, and he thought it worth the risk of a possible spill to stay in her good graces.

"All right, go ahead," he said, "I believe you can do it all right. Be careful when you come to the turn, that's all." Sahwah slid in behind the steering wheel and they started off. The sled traveled faster than it did before, but Sahwah negotiated both the thank—you—marm and the turn with as much skill as Dick himself could have done it, and danced a triumphant war dance when she had brought the bob safely to a stop.

"There now, smarty," she said to the boy who had mistrusted her powers, "you see that a girl can do it as well as a boy."

"You certainly can," said Dick, no less pleased than she herself at her success, "and you may steer the bob the rest of the evening if you want to."

Sahwah engineered two or three more trips and then the excitement lost its tang for her as the element of danger was removed, for the turn had no difficulties for her. "Let's coast down the side of the hill once," she suggested.

"No, thanks," said Migwan, eyeing the steep slope that rose beside the drive.

"Oh, come on," pleaded Sahwah; "it's more fun to go down a steep hill. You go so much faster. It lands you in a snowbank at the bottom, but it's perfectly safe." None of the boys and girls appeared anxious to go. Sahwah jumped up and down with impatience. "Oh, you slowpokes!" she exclaimed, rather crossly. Then she turned to Dick Albright. "Dick," she said, "will you come with me even if the others won't?"

Dick shook his head. "It's dangerous," he answered.

"You're afraid," said Sahwah tauntingly.

"I'm not," said Dick hotly.

"You are too," said Sahwah. "All right if you're afraid, but I know some one who wouldn't be." Now Sahwah had no one definite in mind when she said this last, it was simply an effort to make Dick feel small, but Dick immediately took it as a reference to the unknown Ned Roberts who had sent her the valentine, and his jealousy got the better of his discretion.

"All right," he said, firmly determined to measure up to this pattern of dauntlessness, "come on if you want to. I'll go with you." The two climbed up the steep hill, dragging the bob after them. When Sahwah was sitting behind the steering wheel, poised at the top and ready to make the swift descent, she shuddered at the sight of the sharp incline. It looked so much worse from the top than from the bottom. She would have drawn back and given it up, but Sahwah had a stubborn pride that shrank from saying she was afraid to do anything she had undertaken.

"Shove off!" she commanded, gritting her chattering teeth together. The bob shot downward like a cannon ball. In spite of her terror Sahwah enjoyed the sensation. She held firmly on to the steering wheel and made for the great bank of snow which had been thrown up by the men cleaning the foot walks. At that moment an automobile turned into the lake drive, and its blinding lights shone full into Sahwah's eyes. Dazzled, she turned her head away, at the same time jerking the steering wheel to the right. The bob swerved sharply to one side and crashed into a tree. The force of the impact threw Dick clear of the sled and he rolled head over heels down the hill, landing in the snow at the bottom badly shaken, but otherwise unhurt. Sahwah lay motionless in the snow beside the wreck of the bob.

CHAPTER XII.

DR. HOFFMAN.

The girls and boys crowded around her with frightened faces. "Is she killed?" they asked each other in terrified tones.

"It's all my fault," said Dick Albright, nearly beside himself; "I should have known better than to let her go. She didn't think of the danger, but I did, and I should have prevented her. Was there ever such a fool as I?"

Gladys and Migwan were kneeling beside Sahwah and opening her coat. "She is not dead," said Gladys, feeling her pulse. "We must get her home. She is possibly only stunned." Sahwah moved slightly and groaned, but she did not open her eyes. A passing automobile was hailed and she was carried to it as carefully as possible and taken home.

"A slight concussion of the brain," said the hastily summoned doctor, after he had made his examination, "and a fractured hip. The hip can be fixed all right, but the concussion may be worse than it looks. That is an ugly contusion on her head." The next few days were anxious ones in the Brewster home. Sahwah gave no sign of returning consciousness, and her fever rose steadily. Mrs. Brewster felt her hair turning gray with the suspense, and the Winnebagos could neither eat nor sleep. Poor Dick was frantic, yet he dared not show himself at the house for fear every one would point an accusing finger at him as the one responsible for the misfortune.

But Sahwah, true to her usual habit of always doing the unexpected thing, progressed along just the opposite lines from those prophesied by the physician. After a few days her fever abated and the danger from the concussion was over. Sahwah's head had demonstrated itself to be of a superior solidness of construction. But the hip, which at first had not given them a moment's uneasiness, steadfastly refused to mend. Dr. Benson looked puzzled; then grave. The splintered end of that hip bone began to be a nightmare to him. He called in another doctor for consultation. The new doctor set it in a different way, nearly killing Sahwah with the pain, although she struggled valiantly to be brave and bear it in silence. Nyoda never forgot that tortured smile with which Sahwah greeted her when she came in after the process was over. A week or two passed and the bones still made no effort to knit. Another consulting physician was called in; a prominent surgeon. He ordered Sahwah removed to the hospital, where he made half a dozen X-ray pictures of her hip. The joint was so badly inflamed and swollen that it was impossible to tell just where the trouble lay. Sahwah fumed and fretted with impatience at having to stay in bed so long. Surgeon after surgeon examined the fracture and shook their heads.

At last a long consultation was held, at the close of which Mr. and Mrs. Brewster were called into the council of physicians. "We have discovered," said Dr. Lord, a man high up in the profession who was considered the final authority, "that the ball joint of your daughter's hip has been fractured in such a way that it can never heal. There is one inevitable result of this condition, and that is tuberculosis of the bone. If not arrested this will in time communicate itself to the bones of the upper part of the body and terminate fatally. There is only one way to prevent this outcome and that is amputation of the limb before the disease gets a hold on the system."

"You mean, cut her leg off?" asked Mrs. Brewster faintly.

"Yes," said Dr. Lord shortly. He was a man of few words.

Sahwah was stunned when she heard the verdict of the surgeons. She knew little about disease and it seemed wildly impossible to her that this limb of hers which had been so strong and supple a month ago would become an agent of death if not amputated. She was in an agony of mind. Never to swim again! Never to run and jump and slide and skate and dance! Always to go about on crutches! Before the prospect of being crippled for life her active nature shrank in unutterable horror. Death seemed preferable to her. She buried her face in the pillow in such anguish that the watchers by the bedside could not stand by and see it. After a day of acute mental suffering her old-time courage began to rear its head and she made up her mind that if this terrible thing had to be done she might as well go through with it as bravely as possible. She resigned herself to her fate and urged her parents to give their consent to the operation. Poor Mrs. Brewster was nearly out of her mind with worry over the affair.

"When will you do it?" asked Sahwah, struggling to keep her voice steady.

"In about a week," said Dr. Lord, "when you get a little stronger."

Nyoda went home heartsick from the hospital that day. Sahwah had asked her to write to Dr. Hoffman, her old friend in camp, and tell him the news. With a shaking hand she wrote the letter. "Poor old Dr. Hoffman," she said to herself, "how badly he will feel when he hears that Sahwah is hurt and he can do nothing to help her."

Sahwah had never dreamed how many friends she had until this misfortune overcame her. Boys and girls, as well as old people and little children, horrified at the calamity, came by the dozen to offer cheer and comfort. Her room was filled to overflowing with flowers. Even "old Fuzzytop," whom Sahwah had tormented nearly to death, came to offer his sympathy and present a potted tulip. Stiff and precise Miss Muggins came to say how she missed her from the Latin class. Aunt Phoebe forgave all the jokes she had made at her expense and sent over a crocheted dressing jacket made of fleecy wool.

"Don't feel so badly, Nyoda dear," she said one day as Nyoda sat beside her in the depths of despair. The usual jolly teacher had now no cheery word to offer. The prospect of the gay dancing Sahwah on crutches for the remainder of her life was an appalling tragedy. "I can act out 'The Little Tin Soldier' quite realistically—then," went on Sahwah, her mind already at work to find the humor of the situation. But Nyoda sat staring miserably at the flowers on the dresser.

"Telegram for Miss Brewster," said the nurse, appearing in the doorway.

"A telegram for me?" asked Sahwah curiously, stretching out her hand for the envelope. She tore it open eagerly and read, "Don't operate until I come. Dr. Hoffman." "He's coming!" cried Sahwah. "Dr. Hoffman is coming! He said if I ever broke a bone again he would come and set it! Poor Doctor, how disappointed he'll be when he finds he can't 'set it'!"

Dr. Hoffman arrived the next day.

"Vell, vell, Missis Sahvah," he said anxiously as he saw her lying so ominously still on the bed, "you haf not been trying to push somevon across de top of Lake Erie, haf you?" Sahwah smiled faintly. A ray of sunlight seemed to have entered the room with the doctor, also a gust of wind. He had thrown his hat right into a bouquet of flowers and his hair stood on end and his tie was askew with the haste he had made in getting to the hospital from the train. "Now about this hip, yes?" he said in a businesslike tone. Without any ceremony he brushed the nurse aside and unwrapped the bandages. "Ach so," he said, feeling of the joint with a practised hand, "you did a good job, Missis Sahvah. You make out of your bone a splinter. But vot is dis I hear about operating?" he suddenly exclaimed. "De very idea! Don't you let dem amputate your leg off! Such fool doctors! It's a vonder dey did not cut your head off to cure de bump!" His voice rose to a regular roar. Dr. Lord, coming in at that moment, stopped in astonishment at the sight of this strange doctor standing over his patient. "For vy did you want to amputate her leg off?" shouted Dr. Hoffman at him, dancing up and down in front of him and shaking his finger under his nose. "It is no more diseased dan yours is. And you call yourself a surgeon doctor! Bah! You go out and play in de sunshine and let me take care of dis hip."

"Who the dickens are you?" asked Dr. Lord, looking at him as though he thought he were an escaped lunatic.

"Dis is who I am," replied Dr. Hoffman, handing him a card. "I vas in eighteen-ninety-five by de Staatsklinick in Berlin." Dr. Lord fell back respectfully.

"I know someting about dot Missis Sahvah's bones," went on Dr. Hoffman, "and I know dey vill knit if you gif dem a chance. If all goes vell she vill valk again in t'ree months."

"I'd like to see you do it," said Dr. Lord.

"Patience, my friend," said Dr. Hoffman, "first ve make a little plaster cast." When Mrs. Brewster came in the afternoon she found a strange doctor in command and Dr. Lord and the nurses obeying his orders as if hypnotized. When she went home that night, hope had come to life again in her heart, where it had been dead for more than a week. Dr. Hoffman spent the afternoon having X-ray photographs of the joint made, and sat up all night trying to figure out how those bones could be set so they would knit and still not leave the joint stiff. By morning he had the solution.

The next day—the day the limb was to have been amputated—an operation of a very different nature took place. Dr. Hoffman, looking more like a pastry cook in his operating clothes than anything else, bustled around the operating room keeping the nurses and assisting physicians on the jump.

"Who's the Dutchman that's doing the bossing?" asked a pert young interne of one of the doctors.

"Shut up," answered the doctor addressed, "that's Hoffman, of the Staatsklinick in Berlin, and the Royal College of Vienna. He was Professor of Anatomy in the Staatsklinick '95-'96, don't you remember?" he said, turning to one of the other doctors. "He's a wizard at bonesetting. He performed that operation on Count Esterhazy's youngest son that kept him from being a cripple." The younger doctor looked at Dr. Hoffman with a sudden respect. The case in question was a famous one in surgical annals.

Dr. Lord, angry as he was at Dr. Hoffman's arraignment of him before the nurses and visitors, was yet a big enough man to realize that he had a chance to learn something from this sarcastic intruder who had so unceremoniously taken his case out of his hands, and swallowing his wrath, asked permission to witness the operation. "Ach, yes, to be sure," said Dr. Hoffman, with his old geniality. "You must not mind that I vas so cross yesterday," he went on, "it vas because I vas so impatient ven I hear you vanted to amputate dot girl's leg off. But I forget," he said magnanimously, "you do not know how to set de badly splintered bones so dey vill knit, as I do. Bring all de doctors in you vant to, and all de nurses too. Ve vill haf a Klinick."

Thus it was that the large operating room of the hospital was crowded to the very edge of the "sterile field" with eager medical men, glad of the chance to watch Dr. Hoffman at work. "Who is that young girl in here?" asked Dr. Lord impatiently, as the anaesthetic was about to be administered.

"Some friend of the patient," explained the head nurse. "Hoffman let her in himself." The young girl in question was Medmangi. Dr. Hoffman knew all about her ambition to become a doctor and allowed her to come into the operating room. So she began her career by witnessing one of the most inspired operations of a widely famed surgeon.

When Sahwah came out of the ether she felt as if she were held in a vise. "What's the matter?" she asked dreamily. "I feel so stiff and queer."

"It's the cast they put you in," answered her mother.

Sahwah moved her arms carefully to see if they were in working order yet. Lightly she touched the hard substance that surrounded her hip bone. "They didn't cut it off, did they?" she asked in sudden terror. She could not tell by the feeling whether she had two legs or one.

Dr. Hoffman, coming in in time to hear the question, snorted violently. "Don't talk such nonsense, Missis Sahvah," he said, waving his hands emphatically. "Dot limb is still vere it belongs, and vill be as good as ever ven de cast comes off."

The watchers around the bed that day wore very different expressions from what they had worn all week. Just since yesterday despair had given way to hope and hope to assurance. Her mother and father and Nyoda hovered over the bed with radiant faces, and the Winnebagos, after seeing Sahwah's favorable condition with their own eyes, retired to Gladys's barn to celebrate. The rules of the hospital forbade the amount of noise they felt they must make. Dick Albright smiled his first smile that day since the night of the accident.

CHAPTER XIII.

THE HONOR OF THE WINNEBAGOS.

"For High Style use the Preterite,

For Common use the Past,

In compound verbal tenses

Put the Participle last.

The Perfect Tense with 'Avoir'

With the Subject must agree

(Or does this rule apply to the

Auxiliary 'to be'?)."

Migwan, in high spirits, resolved the rules in her French grammar into poetry as she learned them. Regular lessons were gotten out of the way as quickly as possible these days to give more time to the study of history. And to Migwan studying history meant not merely the memorizing of a number of facts attached to dates which might or might not stay in her mind at the crucial time; it was the bringing to life of bygone races and people, and putting herself in their places, and living along with them the events described on the pages. Taking it in this way, Migwan had a very clear and vivid picture of the things she was learning, and her answers to questions showed such a thorough knowledge of her subject that she was regarded as a "grind" at history, while the truth was that she did less "grinding" than the rest of the class, who merely memorized figures and facts without calling in the aid of the imagination. So Migwan learned her new history and reviewed her old, and was as happy as the day was long.

As the time approached for the examination she felt more sure of herself every day. The long hours of patient study were about to be rewarded, and she would bring honor to the Winnebagos by winning the Parsons prize. That little point about bringing honor to the Winnebagos was keenly felt by Migwan. Ever since Sahwah had covered herself with undying glory in the game with the Carnegie Mechanics, Migwan felt a longing to distinguish herself in some way also. Sahwah's fame was widespread, and when any of the Winnebagos happened to mention that they belonged to that particular group, some one was sure to say, "The Winnebago Camp Fire? Oh, yes, it was one of your number who won the basketball championship for the school by making a record jump for the ball, wasn't it?" The whole group lived in the reflected glory of Sahwah the Sunfish. Now, thought Migwan resolutely, they would have something else to be proud about. In the future people would say, "The Winnebagos? Oh, yes, it was one of your girls who carried off the Parsons prize in history!"

Migwan thrilled with the joy of it, and plunged more deeply into the pages before her. She was a different girl nowadays from the pale, anxious-faced one who had sat up night after night during the winter, desperately trying to add something to the scanty income by the labor of pen and typewriter. Now she was always happy and sparkling, and performed her household tasks with such a will that her languid mother, lying and watching her, was likewise filled with an ambition to be up and doing. She was never cross with Betty these days, no matter how many fits of temper that young lady indulged in. Professor Green often stopped her in the hall to ask her how she was getting along in her preparation, and offered to lend her reference books which would help her in her study. Everybody seemed to be anxious for her to win the prize, and willing to give her all the help possible.

Migwan did not make the mistake of studying until late the night before the examination. She went to bed at nine o'clock, so as to be in fit condition. When she closed her books after the final study she knew all that was to be learned from them. The examination was held in the senior session room after the close of school. Five pupils participated. One was Abraham Goldstein, another was George Curtis, who liked Migwan very well and hated Abraham cordially; the other two were girls. They all sat in one row of seats; Migwan first, then George, then Abraham, and behind him the two girls. The lists of questions were given out. "I hardly need to say," said the teacher in attendance, "that the honor system will be in force during this examination."

Migwan made an effort to still the wild beating of her heart and read the questions through. They all appeared easy to her, as she had had such a thorough preparation. George Curtis groaned to himself as he looked them over, for there were two which he saw at a glance he would be unable to answer. Abraham read his and looked thoughtful. Migwan wrote rapidly with a sure and inspired pen until she came to the last question. There she halted in dismay. The question was in the Ancient History group and read, in part, "Who was the invader of Israel before Sennacherib?" For the life of her she could not think of the name of the Assyrian invader. Last night the whole thing had been as clear as crystal in her mind. She thought until the perspiration stood out on her forehead; she tried every method of suggestion that she knew, but all in vain; the name still eluded her. While she was trying so desperately to recall the name, George Curtis in the seat behind was watching her. By chance he had caught a glimpse of her paper, and saw the figure 10 followed by an empty space, so he knew that it was the tenth question she was having trouble with. This happened to be one he knew and he had just written it out in a bold, black hand. He was out of the race for the prize, for there were two whole questions left out on his sheet. By certain signs of distress from the two girls behind him he knew that they, too, were out, and it now lay between Migwan and Abraham. Abraham was not very well liked by the boys since the affair of the statue. George despised him utterly, and he could not bear to think of his winning that prize.

He watched his chance. It came at last. The teacher dropped her pencil behind her desk, and in the instant when she was picking it up he reached out and pulled Migwan's hair sharply. When she turned around in surprise he framed with his lips the name "Sargon." She understood it perfectly. Then came a mental struggle which matched Sahwah's terrific physical one that day in camp. On one side college stood with its doors wide open to welcome her; she heard the plaudits of her friends who expected and wanted her to win the prize; she saw the joy in her mother's face when she heard the news; she heard the heartfelt congratulations of Nyoda and the Winnebagos who would share in her glory. On the other hand she heard just five ugly words echoing in her ears. "You didn't win it honestly!" She tried to stifle the voice of science. "I knew it perfectly all the time," she said to herself, "and it only slipped my mind for an instant." "But you forgot," said the voice, "and if he hadn't told you you wouldn't have known."

Miserably she argued the question back and forth. It she didn't win the prize Abraham would, and he could well afford to go to college without the money. "He'd cheat if he had the chance," she told herself. "That doesn't help you any," pricked the accuser. "You talk about the honor of the Winnebagos. If you use that information you would be dishonoring the Winnebagos! You're a cheat, you're a cheat," it said tauntingly, and a little sparrow on the window sill outside took up the mocking refrain, "Cheat! Cheat!" Stung as though some one had pointed an accusing finger at her, Migwan flung down her pen in despair and resolutely blotted her paper. She handed in her examination with the last half of the last question unanswered, and fled from the room with unseeing eyes. And in the instant when George was trying to tell Migwan the answer, Abraham, who had also forgotten the name of Sargon, glanced over toward George's paper and saw it written out in his easily readable hand. Without a qualm he wrote it down on his own paper with a triumphant flourish.

There was great surprise throughout the school a few days later when the grades of the examination were made public: Elsie Gardiner, 95; Abraham Goldstein, 98, winner of the Parsons cash prize of $100.

Migwan felt like a wanderer on the face of the earth after losing that history prize. She shrank from meeting the friends who had so confidently expected her to win it, and her own thoughts were too painful to be left alone with. If Hinpoha had been wandering in the Desert of Waiting for the past few months, Migwan was sunk deep in the Slough of Despond. She was at the age when death seemed preferable to defeat, and she wished miserably that she would fall ill of some mortal disease, and never have to face the world again with failure written on her forehead. "Oh, why," she wailed in anguish of spirit, as has many an older and wiser person when confronted with this same unanswerable question, "why was I given this glimpse of Paradise only to have the gate slammed in my face?" That spectre of the winter before, the belief that success would never be hers, gripped her again with its icy hand. And was it any wonder? Twice now the means to enter college had been within her reach, and twice it had been swept away in a single day. But while Migwan was thus learning by hard experience that there is many a slip twixt the cup and the lip, she was also to learn from that same schoolmistress the truth of the old saying, "Three times and out." In the meantime, however, the skies were as gray as the wings of the Thunderbird, and life was like a jangling discord struck on a piano long out of tune.

But even if we would rather be dead than alive, as long as we are alive there remain certain duties which have to be performed regardless of the state of our emotional barometers, and Migwan discovered with a start one day that there were at least a dozen letters in her top bureau drawer waiting to be answered. "It's a shame," she said to herself, as she looked them over. "I haven't written to the Bartletts since last November." The Bartletts were the parents of the little boy who was traced by the aid of her timely snapshot. She opened Mrs. Bartlett's letter and glanced over it to put herself in the mood for answering it. She laughed sardonically as she read. Mrs. Bartlett, confident that Migwan was going to use the reward money to go to college, discussed the merits of different courses, and advised Migwan, above all things, with her talent for writing, to put the emphasis on literature and history. Migwan took a certain grim delight in telling Mrs. Bartlett what had happened to her ambition to go to college. She had a Homeric sense of humor that could see the point when the gods were playing pranks on helpless mortals. She told the story simply and frankly, without any "literary style," such as was usually present in her letters to a high degree; neither did she bewail her lot and seek sympathy, for Migwan was no craven.

Then, having told Mrs. Bartlett that she had made up her mind to give up thoughts of college for several years at least, as her duty to her mother came before her ambition, and had sealed and sent away the letter, it suddenly came over her that the writing she had done all winter and which she now considered a waste of time, had done something for her after all; it had taught her the use of the typewriter, a knowledge which she could turn to account during the summertime, and by working in an office somewhere, she could possibly earn enough money to enter college in the fall after all. And up went Migwan's spirits again, like a jack-in-the-box, and went soaring among the clouds like the swallows.

CHAPTER XIV.

AN AUTOMOBILE AND A DRIVER.

Along in the last week of May, Nyoda, on a shopping tour downtown, dropped into a restaurant for a bit of lunch. As she was sitting down to the table, another young woman came and sat down opposite her. The two glanced at each other.

"Why, Elizabeth Kent!" exclaimed the latest arrival.

"Why, Norma Williamson!" exclaimed Nyoda, recognizing an old college friend.

"Not Norma Williamson any more," said the friend, blushing as she drew off her glove and displayed the rings on her fourth finger; "Norma Bates."

"What are you doing to pass the time away?" asked the pretty little matron when she had exhausted her own experiences of the last few years. Nyoda told her about her teaching and the guardianship of the Winnebagos. "Camp Fire Girls?" said Mrs. Bates. "How delightful! I think that is one of the best things that ever happened to girls. If I were not so frightfully busy I would take a group too—I may yet. But I wish you would bring your girls out to visit us. We're living on the Lake Shore for the summer. Camp Fire Girls would certainly know how to have a good time at our place. We have a launch and a sailboat and horses to ride and a tennis court. Can't you come out next Saturday?" Nyoda thought perhaps they could. "I'll tell you what to do," said Mrs. Bates, warming to the scheme. "Come out Friday after school and stay until Sunday night. That will give the girls more chance to do things. We have plenty of room."

"The same hospitable Norma Williamson as of old," said Nyoda, smiling at her. "Don't you remember how we girls used to flock to your room in college, and when it was apparently as fall as it could get you would always make room for one more?"

"I love to have people visit me," said Mrs. Bates simply.

"By the way," said Nyoda, as she rose to depart, "how do you get to

Bates Villa?"

"Take the Interurban car," replied Mrs. Bates, "and get off at Stop 42. The Limited leaves the Interurban Station at four o'clock; that would be a good car to come on."

"All right," said Nyoda, extending her hand in farewell; "we'll be there."

The news of the invitation to spend a week-end in the country was received with a shout by the Winnebagos. Their only regret was that Sahwah would be unable to go. "Never mind, Sahwah," comforted Nyoda, "Mrs. Bates wants us to come out again when the water is warm enough to go in bathing and by that time your hip will be all right."

On Friday, after school was out, Nyoda and Gladys left the building together. "You are coming home with me, as we planned, until it is time to take the car?" asked Nyoda.

"I'm afraid I'll have to go home first, after all," said Gladys. "I came away in such a hurry this morning that I forgot my sweater and my tennis shoes and I really must have them. You come home with me."

But on arriving at the Evans house they found nobody home. Gladys rang and waited and rang again, but there was no answer. Gladys frowned with vexation. "I simply must have that sweater and those shoes," she said. "There's no use in waiting until some one comes home; it'll be too late. Mother has gone for the day and father is out of town, and if Katy has been given a day off she won't be at home until evening. We'll have to break into the house, that's all there is to it."

Feeling like burglars, they tried all the windows on the first floor and the basement. Everything was locked tightly. Gladys began to feel desperate. "Do you suppose I had better break the pantry window," she asked, "or possibly one of the cellar ones? I'll pay for it out of my allowance. I think the pantry window would be the best, because the door at the head of the cellar stairs is likely to be locked and we might not be able to get upstairs if we did get into the cellar."

Nyoda was inspecting the upper windows of the house. "There is one open a little," she said; "the one over the side entrance." Gladys abandoned her idea of breaking the pantry window and bent her energies to reaching the open one. With the aid of Nyoda she climbed up the post of the little side porch, swung herself over the edge of the roof and raised the window.

"Stop where you are!" called a commanding voice. Gladys and Nyoda both started guiltily. A man was running across the lawn from the next estate. "Stop or I'll call the police," he said, coming upon the drive.

He looked much disconcerted when Nyoda and Gladys both burst into a ringing peal of laughter. "Oh, it's too funny for anything," said Gladys, wiping her eyes, "to be caught breaking into your own house. You're a good man, whoever you are, for keeping an eye on the house," she said to the puzzled-looking arrester, "but the joke is on you this time. This is my father's house. I'm Gladys Evans. Give him one of my cards out of my purse, Nyoda, so he'll believe it."

"I beg your pardon," said the man, convinced that Gladys had a right to enter the Evans's house by the second-story window if she chose. "I'm the new gardener next door and I didn't know you, and it always looks suspicious to see such goings-on."

"You did perfectly right," said Gladys, as he went back to his work.

Laughing extravagantly over their being taken for housebreakers, Gladys climbed into the window and went downstairs. Opening the front door a crack, she gave a low whistle which she fondly believed to be a burglar-like signal. Nyoda answered with a similar whistle. "Is that you, Diamond Dick?" she asked in a thrilling whisper.

"Who stands without?" asked Gladys.

"It is I, Dark-lantern Pete," hissed Nyoda.

"Give the countersign," commanded Gladys.

"Six buckets of blood!" replied Nyoda in a curdling voice.

Gladys admitted her into the house and they both sat down on the stairs and shrieked with laughter. "Oh, I can hardly wait until we get down to the car, so we can tell the other girls," said Gladys. "Caught in the act! My fair name is ruined. Now for some dinner."

"I'm hungry for a pickle," she said as they foraged in the pantry for something to eat. "Wait a minute until I go down cellar and get some." As she opened the door of the cool cellar she started back in surprise. On the floor lay Katy, the maid, unconscious. An overturned chair beside her and a shattered light globe told how she had tried to screw a new bulb into the fixture in the ceiling and had tipped over with the chair, striking her head on the cement floor. "Nyoda, come down here," called Gladys. Nyoda hastened down. Together they laid the unconscious girl on a pile of carpet and tried to revive her. After a few minutes' work Nyoda went upstairs and called the ambulance to take Katy to the hospital. When she had been examined by a surgeon and pronounced badly stunned but not seriously injured, Gladys and Nyoda breathed a sigh of relief and left her in the care of the hospital.

"We've had enough excitement to-day to last a month," said Gladys, as they hastened tack to the house the second time to get the sweater and shoes. "I'm all tired out."

"So am I," said Nyoda.

"We have just time enough to make that four o'clock car, and none to spare," said Gladys, as they rode toward town in the street-car. As if everything were conspiring against them to-day, a heavy truck, loaded with boxes, got caught in the car-track right in front of them and blocked traffic for ten minutes. Gladys and Nyoda looked tragically at each other at this delay. Nyoda held up her watch significantly. It was ten minutes to four. Just then Gladys spied a man she knew in an automobile, slowly passing the car. She called to him through the open window. "Will you take us in if we get off the car?" she asked. "We're trying to make the four o'clock Limited."

"Certainly," agreed the obliging friend. The transfer of seats was soon made. "How much time have you?" asked the friend as he shoved in the spark.

"Ten minutes," replied Gladys.

"We'll make it," said the friend, dodging between the vehicles that were standing around the disabled truck, helping to pull it from the car-tracks. Getting into a clear road, he opened the throttle and they proceeded like the wind for about six blocks. Then, for no apparent reason, the car slowed down, and with a whining whir of machinery came to a dead stop. "I'm afraid I can't make good my promise to catch that car," said the friend in a vexed tone, after vainly trying to start the car for several minutes. "I'll have to be towed to a garage," Nyoda and Gladys jumped out, hailed a passing street-car and reached the station just five minutes too late. The Limited had already pulled out.

"Five girls with red ties?" repeated the crossing policeman when they made inquiries to find out if the other girls had gone and left them. "They all got on the Limited." There was no doubt about their having gone, then.

"You know, you said if any were late they'd get left," said Gladys. "Whoever was here for the car was to go and not wait. Won't they laugh, though, at you being the late one?"

"There won't be another Limited for two hours," said Nyoda impatiently, "and the local takes twice as long to get there. I'll telephone Mrs. Bates that we missed this car but will come out on the next Limited."

"Missed the car?" said Mrs. Bates, when they had her on the wire. "That's too bad. But you won't have to wait for the other Limited. Our driver is in town to-day with the automobile and he can bring you out. He's in Morrison's now ordering some supplies, and the car is at the corner of —— th Avenue and L—— Street. Just get into the car and it'll be all right. John always calls me up before he starts for home and I'll tell him about you. It's a blue car, rather bright, with a cane streamer."

Much cheered by the thought of an automobile ride through the country instead of a two-hour wait and the prospect of being packed like sardines into the crowded interurban car, Nyoda and Gladys moved down to the corner of ——th Avenue and L—— Street and found the car just as Mrs. Bates had said. With a sigh of comfort they settled down on the cushions. "Our struggles are over," said Nyoda, leaning back luxuriously and counting over the various things that had happened to them since leaving school at noon. In a few moments the driver appeared, touched his hat respectfully to the two girls in the tonneau, and got into the front seat without any comment. He had his orders from Mrs. Bates.

"It's just like Norma Williamson to have a blue car with blue cushions," said Nyoda, as they sped through the streets toward the city limits. "She was always so fond of blue in college. And this cane streamer is just the finishing touch. She always liked things trimmed up gaily. It's a pleasant thing for the Winnebagos that I met her that day. She'll be a regular fairy godmother to us." Talking happily about the fun they would have on this week-end party, they rode along the pleasant country roads, bordered with flowering apple trees, and drank in the sweet-scented air with unbounded delight. "Could anything be lovelier than the country in May?" sighed Nyoda.

"Wouldn't it be a joke," said Gladys, "if we were to get there ahead of the others, after missing the car? Wouldn't they stare, though, to find us waiting for them? We must be nearly there now." The automobile left the main road and turned down toward the lake. "That must be the place," continued Gladys, as a white house came into view far in the distance.

"I don't see any of the girls waiting for us," said Nyoda. "I declare, I believe we're here first. Oh, what a joke!" The estate through which they were driving was a very large one, much of it covered with great trees. The house was painted white, and perched directly on the edge of the cliff. The automobile halted before the porch and Nyoda and Gladys got out. A woman, evidently a servant, came to the screen door and held it open, motioning them to come in. Neither Mrs. Bates nor any of the girls were in evidence. The servant said nothing.

"I believe they're all hiding on us!" said Nyoda, getting a sudden light on this apparently neglectful reception. "I know Norma's tricks of old. If we could only think of some way to turn the laugh on them!" The servant who had admitted them led the way to an inner room and opened a door, stepping aside to let them go first. Then she followed and closed the door after them. They found that they were in an elevator. The woman pushed a button and they began to rise. "Of all things, an elevator in a country house!" said Gladys. They rose to a height which must have equalled the third story of the house, although they passed no open floor. They came to a halt before an opening covered with an iron grating. To the girls it looked like the ordinary elevator entrance. At a touch from the woman the grating moved aside and they stepped out into the room. The elevator descended noiselessly and Nyoda and Gladys were alone.

"It's a tower room!" said Gladys. The chamber they were in was square, about fifteen by fifteen, furnished as a bedroom. Through a door which opened at one side they could see a luxurious tiled bath. The walls and ceiling of the chamber were tinted a deep violet, and the covers on the bed, dresser, table and the upholstery of the chairs were of the same shade. The lamp globes hanging from the ceiling were deep purple.

"What an extraordinary color to decorate a room in," said Nyoda. "I wonder if this is where we are going to sleep. Where can Mrs. Bates be, I wonder?" she said, getting rather impatient for the joke to be sprung.

Just at this time Gladys made a discovery. There was only one window in the room, curtained with heavy cretonne, purple, to match the rest of the hangings. Drawing the curtain aside to look out at the landscape, she suddenly stood still, frozen to the spot. At her exclamation Nyoda turned around and also stood as if turned to stone. The window was barred! "What does it mean?" asked Gladys in a horrified voice. The two hastened back to the elevator entrance and looked for the button to summon the elevator. There was none. They called down the shaft repeatedly, but there was no answer. As they stood listening for sounds from below they heard the automobile which had brought them start up and drive away from the house. After that there was not another sound of any kind. An unnamable terror seized them both. Each read the other's fear in her eyes. Rushing to the window, they looked out. There was nothing to be seen but the lake stretching out before them, calm and smiling in the May sunshine. The boom of the waves sounded directly beneath them, and they knew that the tower was on the extreme edge of the bluff.

"This is not Norma Bates's house," said Nyoda in a frightened voice.

"She said that they were a hundred feet back from the lake."

"Whose house is it, then?" asked Gladys.

"I can't imagine," said Nyoda. "It's all a mistake somewhere."

"But that was the Bates's automobile, all right, that we got into," said

Gladys.

"Yes," said Nyoda reflectively; "bright blue with a cane streamer, standing at the corner of ——th Avenue and L—— Street. But was it the right one?" she asked suddenly, putting her hands to her head. "That driver never said a word, just got in and drove off. What on earth are we into?"

Gladys's face suddenly went as white as chalk. "Nyoda!" she gasped, clutching the other girl's arm.

"What is it?" asked Nyoda.

"You read every day in the papers of girls disappearing," said Gladys faintly, "never to be heard of again. Have we—have we—disappeared?"

"I don't know," said Nyoda, with thoughts whirling. She turned away from the window, toward the elevator. Not a sound of any kind had been heard, and yet when she turned around there was the elevator up again with the same woman in it who had brought them up. Instead of opening the door, however, she pressed something and a little slide opened at about the height of her head. Through this she passed a supper tray, which she set on a shelf on the wall at the side of the elevator. Gladys and Nyoda hastened toward her.

"What is the meaning of this?" asked Nyoda. The woman made no answer. "In whose house are we?" demanded Nyoda. Still no reply. "Answer me," said Nyoda sharply. The woman pointed to her ears and shook her head, then pointed to her lips and shook her head. "She's deaf and dumb!" exclaimed Nyoda. The woman pressed a button and the elevator sank from sight.

Nyoda and Gladys faced each other in consternation. The mystery was becoming deeper. Beyond a doubt they were not in Mrs. Bates's house; beyond a doubt they were the victims of some mistake; but how was the mistake to be cleared up if they could not make themselves understood? They looked the room over thoroughly for some clew to the mystery. They found none. There was no door leading from the room except the one opening into the bath. There was no door leading out from the bath, to any other room; neither was there any window. The little room was lighted by electricity. As in the other room, everything here was violet-colored. The tiled walls, the floor, the calcimined ceiling, the light globe, the enameled medicine chest, the outside of the bathtub, and even a little three-legged stool, were all the same shade. The wonder of the girls increased momentarily.

"Can this be real," asked Nyoda, looking around her in a daze, "or are we in the middle of some nightmare? Pinch me to see if I'm awake."

"We're awake, all right," said Gladys.

"Then have we dropped back into one of the novels of Dumas? Can this be the year 1915? Imprisoned in a lonely tower, with no window except one over the lake, and that window barred. How did we get here, anyway?" she asked wearily, her head spinning with the effort to make head or tail out of their position. "Let's see, just how was it? We missed the Limited, telephoned Mrs. Bates, and she told us that her automobile was at the corner of ——th Avenue and L—— Street—a bright blue automobile with a cane streamer—and we should get in and the driver would come and take us out to Bates Villa. We went down to the corner, found the automobile, got in, and the driver came and drove off and we landed here." Her temples throbbed as she tried to recall anything out of the way in the business. But no light came. The whole thing was mysterious, inexplicable, grotesque.

"Hadn't we better eat something?" suggested Gladys gently. "It evidently isn't their intention to starve us, whatever they are keeping us here for."

"You are right," said Nyoda, and she lifted the tray down from the shelf. The dishes and silver were of good quality, but the knives were so dull that it was impossible to cut anything with them. After vainly trying to make an impression on a piece of meat, Gladys threw her knife aside impatiently.

"They certainly never made those knives to cut with," she said.

At her remark Nyoda raised her head suddenly. She thought she saw a ray of light on the situation. "Gladys," she said, "do you know what kind of people they give dull knives to? It's insane people! This room was undoubtedly designed for some one afflicted in that way. That is why the window is barred, and there is no door, and why the room is done in lavender. Lavender has a soothing and depressing effect on people's nerves and would probably keep an insane person from becoming violent. We got here through some awful mistake."

Gladys shuddered violently. "How horrible!" she said. "I suppose that woman actually considers us insane. How long do you suppose they will keep us here?"

"Only until they find out their mistake," answered Nyoda, "which I hope will be soon. I shall write a note and give it to the woman when she comes up again."

Both their spirits revived when they arrived at this theory, and they returned to their supper with good appetites. "I wish I could cut this meat," sighed Gladys. Then she brightened. "I have my Wohelo knife in my handbag," she said, rising and going over to the bed where her coat lay. She stopped in disappointment when she opened the bag. The knife was not there. "I remember now," she said; "I took it out just before we left home and must have forgotten to put it back in again, we left in such a hurry."

"What will the girls think, anyway, when we fail to arrive at the

Bates's?" said Nyoda.

"They'll probably telephone to town," said Gladys, "and mother will know I didn't get there and she will be frantic." She lost all her appetite with a rush when this thought came to her.

They waited impatiently for the return of the woman with the tray. Nyoda wrote a note and had it ready for her. It read:

"There has been some mistake. We are not the persons you intended to keep here."

But the woman did not come. Darkness fell outside the window and they lighted the lights in the room, but still there was no movement of the elevator. They spent the evening pacing up and down the room, discussing the mysterious situation in which they found themselves, until from sheer weariness they lay down on the bed. They did not undress and they left the lights burning, intending to watch for the return of the woman. They set the tray on the floor at some distance from the elevator.

"Can it be possible," said Gladys, "that it was only this afternoon that we broke into our house? It seems years ago." Nyoda lay staring at the elevator shaft, awaiting the return of the cage.

"This purple glare over everything hurts my eyes," she said. She closed them a minute to get relief. When she opened them again there was a broad streak of light coming in through the window. The lights were out in the room and the tray had disappeared from the floor. Gladys lay sound asleep, her head pillowed on her arm. Nyoda started up and was on the point of rousing Gladys. "No, I'll let her sleep," she thought; "it's a good thing she can."

She went to the window and looked out through the bars at the sun rising over the water. There was the same old lake with which she had been familiar all her life, with the cliffs jutting out in points, one always a little farther out than the other, to form the great curve of the shore line. She must have passed this place dozens of times while riding in the lake boats. Here was a scene she had admired many times from the open shore, and now she was looking at it from behind bars, a prisoner. It was too grotesque to be true. She turned pensively toward the bed and noticed with a start that a tray containing breakfast for two stood on the shelf beside the elevator. And yet she had not heard a sound! Gladys was still asleep on the bed. As Nyoda stood looking down at her she woke up and stared around the room uncomprehendingly. She could not place herself at first. Then at the sight of the violet room the events of yesterday came back to her.

They ate breakfast with what appetite they could and then sat down close beside the elevator shaft to be sure and see the deaf-mute when she came, for it seemed impossible to detect her visit when they had their backs turned. While they waited they examined the iron grating for the door opening, but found none. There was apparently no break in the scroll-work anywhere, no hinge, no slide arrangement. "Did we come into the room through there, or did we only imagine it?" asked Nyoda, completely baffled. "Surely we didn't come through that little grating that opens on top, did we? I declare, I'm getting so bewildered that if any one told us we did come in that way I wouldn't dispute them."

Almost while she was speaking the elevator cage shot rapidly and noiselessly into view and the deaf-mute opened the slide to take the tray. Instead of giving it to her, however, they gave her the note first. She took it and read it and then looked at the two girls in silence. "Maybe she would write something if you gave her a pencil," suggested Gladys.

Nyoda handed the woman a pencil through the iron scroll-work. She wrote something on the bottom of the paper and handed it back to Nyoda. Nyoda took the piece of paper and read:

"There is no mistake about your being here."

As she stood in open-mouthed astonishment the elevator sank from view.

CHAPTER XV.

THE ESCAPE.

"No mistake about our being here!" gasped Nyoda. Her knees failed her and she sank weakly to the floor. "What can that mean? Are we kidnapped? Do you suppose we are being held for ransom?"

"It's too horrible," said Gladys, passing her hand over her eyes. "Such things happen in novels, but not in real life."

"And yet," said Nyoda musingly, "if you read the newspapers, you see that stranger things happen in reality than in fiction."

"If we're being held for ransom," said Gladys, "then mother and father will find out where I am." She was more troubled about the worry her disappearance would cause her parents than about any evil which might befall herself.

They rushed to the window to see if any boat was passing which they could signal. Not a sign of anything. Whoever had constructed this tower had considered a great many things. Built in the middle of an extensive estate and hidden on three sides by tall trees, it was not visible from the road at all. The barred window in the tower could only be seen from the lake side, so that if some one should wander through the grounds the appearance of the house itself would excite no suspicion. At some distance on each side of the tower a long rocky pier extended far out into the water. It was not a landing pier, for the rocks were piled unevenly on each other. These rocks changed the current of the water and made boating in the vicinity dangerous, so that launches and sailboats gave the place a wide berth. Then, on the outside of the barred window, clearing it by about two feet, there was an ornamental wooden trellis on which vines grew, which effectually screened the barred window from detection on the lake side.

All these excellent points of construction were borne in on the girls as they circled the room again and again looking for some way of escape. Discouraged and heartsick, they finally sat down on the bed and faced each other When the woman brought their dinner they made a further attempt to get from her the meaning of their being held there, but in vain. To all their written questions she simply wrote,

"I can tell you nothing."

The afternoon dragged slowly by, the girls getting more dejected all the time.

"I believe this violet color is affecting me already," said Nyoda. "I never felt so depressed and melancholy."

"It's the same way with me," said Gladys.

"If there was only one bright spot to relieve the monotony," said Nyoda, "it wouldn't be so bad."

"How about our middy ties?" asked Gladys. "They're bright red and ought to inspire courage." She took the ties from her little satchel and spread them out over a chair.

"That's better," said Nyoda. "I feel more cheerful already." After staring intently at the flaming square of silk for a while her mental activity began to revive and she commenced to turn over in her mind plans for their escape. Acting on this latest impulse, she wrote a letter addressed to a friend of hers and sealed and stamped it. When the deaf-mute brought their supper she drew a diamond ring from her finger, laid it beside the letter and wrote on a piece of paper,

"The ring is yours if you will mail this letter."

The woman shook her head. Nyoda drew off another ring, a handsome ruby surrounded by seed pearls and tiny diamonds. The woman gazed steadfastly at it, and Nyoda thought she saw a longing look in her eyes. She turned the ring so the stone sparkled in the light. The woman's lips parted and her hand crept toward the letter. Nyoda turned the ring in the light once more. By the look in the woman's face she knew that she had gained her point. In another moment she would accept the bribe. Just then the throbbing sound of a motor was heard on the drive. The woman started violently, jerked her hand back and sent the elevator down in haste. With a gesture of despair Nyoda threw the letter down on the dresser.

"Do you suppose she really is deaf?" asked Gladys. "She seemed to hear that sound."

"Maybe she heard it," said Nyoda, "and then again she may have felt the vibrations. Who do you suppose has come?"

They spent the evening in a thrill of expectation, but were undisturbed. Without lighting the lights they stood looking at the stars through the openings in the trellis. At last Nyoda turned from the window and snapped on the switch. As she did so she noticed that the elevator cage had been up and was just going down. As it sank out of sight she saw that the occupant was a man. Soon afterward they heard the throb of the motor again and then the sound of a car driving away.

"Where did you put the red ties?" asked Gladys the next morning.

"I didn't take them," said Nyoda. The ties had disappeared from the chair overnight.

From sheer nervousness Nyoda began twisting up her felt outing hat in her hands. As she did so she came upon something hard in the inside of the crown. Investigating she drew out her Wohelo knife. "I had forgotten I had it in there," she said. "I put that pocket in my hat just for fun and slipped the knife in to see if it would go in."

Why is it that a knife in one's hand inspires a desire to cut something? Nyoda immediately began examining the room for a possible means of escape with the aid of the knife. Opening the window, she inspected the setting of the bars closely. They were set only into the wooden window sill. "Gladys," she whispered excitedly, "I believe we can cut the wood away from these bars and push them out."

"And what then?" asked Gladys.

"Jump," said Nyoda. "Jump into the lake and swim away."

Not daring to make any attempt in the daytime for fear of the mysteriously silent visits of the deaf-mute, who never came at any regular time, they waited until after dark, and then Gladys sat close beside the elevator shaft, watching for the slightest indication of the approaching car. Nyoda meanwhile hacked away at the window casing, cutting and splitting it away from the bars. She worked feverishly for several hours and succeeded in freeing the ends of three of the bars, which would be enough to let them through. Just then Gladys gave a warning hiss. The elevator cord was moving. Nyoda drew the shade down over the window and closed the purple curtains over it, and both girls jumped into bed and pulled the covers over them. They had undressed so as to avert suspicion. The next moment the elevator door opened silently, but whether it moved up or down or side wise they could not make out, and the deaf-mute stepped into the room. Guided by a flash-light, she picked up Gladys's red petticoat from the chair and departed as silently as she had come. As soon as the elevator had sunk out of sight the girls were back at work again. Throwing all her weight against the bars, Nyoda bent them out and upward, the wood that held them at the top splintering with the strain. Then, leaning out, she began to cut away the trellis, which was in the way. It was built out from the sill and had no supports on the ground, and the vines which were on it came around the corner of the house.

Looking down, she could see that they were indeed right above the lake, without a foot of ground at the bottom of the tower. No other part of the house was visible from this angle. The waves roared and dashed on the cliff below, and a strong wind was blowing from the west. "It looks as if a storm were coming," said Nyoda in a low tone. The night was wearing away fast and the girls knew that it was safer to escape under cover of darkness. About three o'clock in the morning the storm broke, a terrific thunder shower. The tower swayed in the wind and at each crash they held their breath, thinking that the house had been struck. The spray from the waves as they were flung against the rocks often came in through the open window. Both girls looked down into the boiling sea beneath them and drew back with a shudder. "Wait until the storm is over," said Gladys.

"It may be daylight then," said Nyoda. Howling like an imprisoned giant, the wind hurled itself against the side of the tower. "There's one thing about it," said Nyoda, "we never can swim in those waves with skirts on. I'm going to have a bathing suit." Taking the blankets from the bed, she made them into straight narrow sacks, cutting various holes in them so as to leave the arms and limbs free.

When the storm had abated somewhat they prepared for the plunge. The first faint streaks of dawn were showing in the east. Gladys crept out on the sill and then shrank back. The surface of the water seemed miles below her. "I can't do it, Nyoda," she panted.

"Yes, you can," said Nyoda, patting her on the shoulder. "You aren't going to lose your nerve at this stage of the game, are you? 'Screw your courage to the sticking point,' We have our fate in our own hands now. 'Who hesitates is lost.'"

"But the water is so far away," shuddered Gladys.

"What of that?" said Nyoda. "It's perfectly safe to jump. The water is very deep along the shore here. Think, just one leap and then we're out of this!"

Gladys still hung back. "You go first," she pleaded.

Nyoda made a motion to go and then stopped. "No," she said firmly, "I'd rather you went first. You might be afraid to follow me afterward. Brace up; remember you're a Winnebago!"

This had its effect and without allowing herself to stop to think Gladys tossed her bundle of clothes out of the window and, closing her eyes, dropped from the sill. There was a wild moment of suspense as she sank downward through the gloom, and then she struck the water and it rolled over her head. It was icy cold and for a minute she felt numb. Then the waves parted over her head and she felt the wind blowing against her face. A great splash beside her terrified her for an instant, and then she remembered that it was Nyoda jumping in after her. In a moment a head came up nearby and Nyoda inquired calmly how she enjoyed the bathing. "It's g-r-r-e-a-t," said Gladys with chattering teeth.

"Now for a little pleasure swim," said Nyoda, striking out. While they were swimming away the storm broke the second time; the thunder sounded in their ears like cannon and the vivid lightning flashes lit up the shore for miles around. By its light they could see that they were nearing one of the long stone piers. Climbing up on this, they rested until they had their breath back again, although it was a rather exciting rest, for the waves were going high over the pier and threatened to wash them off every moment. The shore line along here was peculiarly rugged and forbidding. Instead of a beach, high cliffs rose perpendicularly out of deep water and afforded nowhere a landing place. The girls swam slowly and easily, fearing to spend their strength before they could reach shallow water, often turning over to float and gain a few moments' rest in this way. The waves were very rough and tossed them about a great deal, but the wind was west and they were swimming toward the east, and as the natural current of the lake was eastward toward Niagara, their progress was helped rather than retarded by the force of the water.

The storm abated and the sun began to rise over the lake, gilding the crest of the waves. Still no sign of a beach. "I can't go much further," said Gladys faintly. Both girls were nearly spent when Nyoda spied a strip of yellow in the distance which put new strength into them. Putting forth their last efforts, they headed toward it. Trembling with weakness and breathless from being buffeted about so much, they gained the narrow beach and with a great sigh of relief rolled out onto the sand.

CHAPTER XVI.

A SCHEME AND WHAT CAME OF IT.

We will now have to take our readers away from the Winnebagos and their affairs for a few moments and admit them into the private office of Mr. Rumford Thurston. Mr. Thurston, dealer in stocks and bonds and promoter of investments, was closeted with his business associate and intimate friend, Mr. Nathan Scovill. An earnest discussion was in progress, the theme of which was apparently drawn from a paper which was spread out on the desk between them.

"I tell you, it's the chance of a lifetime," said Mr. Scovill. "We can clean up a cool half million on it before the public wakes up, and when they do we can take a trip to Hawaii or Manila for our health until the business is forgotten. You put in ten thousand now and you'll be on easy street for the rest of your life."

"But I tell you, I haven't the ten thousand to put in," answered Mr.

Thurston crossly. "I haven't one thousand. That last deal finished me."

"Borrow some," said Mr. Scovill impatiently.

"Can't get any more credit," said Mr. Thurston gloomily. "The office furniture is attached already."

Mr. Scovill scowled. Then he went carefully over the ground again, dwelling on the ease of making money without working for it by the simple method of swindling the public, and enlarging on the joys of life as a rich man. "Think, man," he said in conclusion, "think what you're missing!"

Mr. Thurston leaned his head on his hands and thought of what he was missing, and he also thought of something else. A peculiar calculating expression appeared in his eyes and around the corners of his mouth. "There is some money to be had," he said slowly, "if I can get hold of it."

"Where?" asked Mr. Scovill eagerly. "If it's to be had you may rest assured we'll get hold of it by hook or crook."

"You remember John Rogers?" asked Mr. Thurston. Mr. Scovill nodded.

"When he died he left his daughters a fortune in stocks," continued Mr.

Thurston.

"Yes?" inquired Mr. Scovill encouragingly.

"Well," said Mr. Thurston, with a glitter in his eye, "I was appointed guardian of those two girls."

Mr. Scovill whistled. "Meaning to say———" he began.

"That I have the managing of their property until they come of age," finished Mr. Thurston.

"Our fortune's made," said Mr. Scovill, shaking him by the hand.

"The only thing is," said Mr. Thurston, scratching his head reflectively, "that the oldest girl comes of age in June, and there might be an awkward inquiry just at the wrong time. We can't afford to have any investigations begun inside of the next six months if we expect to carry through the other scheme. Any breath of scandal would wreck our prospects."

Mr. Scovill's face fell. He saw only too clearly the truth of the other's words. But where Mr. Thurston came to a halt in front of a dead wall, Scovill's scheming mind saw the loophole. "But just suppose," he said slowly, "that there shouldn't be any investigation when the oldest girl comes of age? Suppose she should never put in a claim for her property?"

"What do you mean?" asked Mr. Thurston.

"Something like this," said Mr. Scovill. "If she were to be kept shut up somewhere for a year or so until you have had time to make your fortune, it would be too late to hurt you with a disclosure after that. Where nobody asks questions there is no need of answering."

Thurston saw the point, but he didn't see how it was going to be done. It was Scovill who thought out the whole scheme. He had a large piece of land far outside the city limits on the lake front. There was an unoccupied house on the property. Here the girl could be kept locked up on the pretext that she was insane, with a certain woman he knew as keeper, a deaf-mute. He shared a secret with her and could use this knowledge to force her to serve him. The whole thing was very simple.

"But how are we going to keep the one locked up away from the other?" asked Mr. Thurston. "Her sister would have the whole country searching for her."

"Then take them both," said Mr. Scovill promptly. "That'll make matters simpler yet. You say they have no relatives and are now away in school? Nothing could be easier. We'll build a room they can't get out of once they're in, and when it's finished you invite them to your house for a visit. They'll think they're coming to see you, but it's out there to that house they'll go and they'll not come back in a hurry. In the meantime you get hold of those stocks and bonds, sell them and put the money in this venture and come out a rich man. When you're ready to clear out of the country you can let the girls out, and they won't be any worse off than when they went in— except that they won't have a cent."

Bit by bit the plan was perfected. Mr. Thurston took a sudden interest in his orphan wards to the extent of writing to the school where they were attending and asking when it closed for the summer. When he was informed that school closed the last week in May, he invited the two girls, Genevieve and Antoinette Rogers, to spend the first weeks of their vacation at his home. He had not seen either of them since they were little children. They graciously accepted the invitation.

But on the day they were to arrive, Mr. Thurston found that some private business of his very urgently required his presence in another city, and left Mr. Scovill to see to the landing of the birds in the trap. Mr. Scovill met the unsuspecting girls at the train, explaining with many expressions of regret the enforced absence of their guardian, took them to dinner in a fine hotel and showed them the sights of the town with all the cordiality of a sincere friend of their host, who was doing his best to make up for his not being there. He won their hearts completely. They were simple girls who had been brought up in a strict church school, and the sights and sounds of the large city were all wonderful to them.

Now, thanks to Mr. Scovill's activities, the trap was all set. The tower was built with its room at the top without any door and its barred window, and the deaf-mute was installed on the place and given instructions to act as guard to two girls who were mentally unbalanced. Furnishing the room in violet was the last touch of his cunning brain, because he knew the depressing effect it would have on the inmates. He gave strict orders to the keeper to remove any sign of a bright color, as this might cause them to become violent.

Mr. Scovill had left directions for his automobile to be at a certain place at half-past four to convey them to the house in the country. Now, for reasons of his own, Mr. Scovill did not wish to be the last one seen in the company of the two girls in case his plans should go wrong and some one would start an inquiry for them. Therefore, he gave his driver private instructions to drive like the wind with two girls who should be placed in the car, and under no condition to let them out of the car.

Accordingly, when they were all a little weary of sight-seeing he steered them gently toward the corner of ——th Avenue and L—— Street, where the car was to wait for them. Half a block off he saw that it was in place. So, pulling out his watch and suddenly remembering that he had an important engagement for that very minute, he courteously took his leave and pointed out the car they were to get into, telling them that it was Mr. Thurston's and would take them to his home. "You can't miss it, girls," he said, pointing with his finger. "It's that bright blue one with the basket-work streamer." Antoinette and Genevieve thanked him kindly for showing them such a good time and entered the car he had indicated. Mr. Scovill withdrew into a doorway and watched them. In a few moments the driver appeared, saw the two girls in the machine, touched his hat to them, and taking his place behind the wheel, drove rapidly off in the opposite direction. Mr. Scovill rubbed his hands together as he watched the car disappear. It was a way he had when his plans were turning out nicely. Forty-five minutes later his driver called up from the country house to say that he had brought the girls out in safety. Mr. Scovill smiled blandly. So far everything had played into his hands. When Mr. Thurston returned the following day he announced the fact to him that the birds were safe in the trap. Then he left town for a protracted stay. Mr. Thurston made one trip out to the house to behold the thing for himself. Riding up in the elevator, he saw the girls standing by the barred window of their prison. When they lit the light he descended in haste so as not to be seen by them. Then he also left town for a while.

The Winnebagos, who were all in time for the Limited except Nyoda and Gladys, boarded the car without them and amused themselves during the ride by thinking up ways to tease the tardy ones when they should arrive on the next car. Pretty Mrs. Bates met them at the car stop with the news that Nyoda and Gladys were coming out in the automobile, and when they thought it was time for them to arrive they all lined up in the road where the drive turned off, and were ready to sing a funny song which Migwan had made up about not getting there on time. The blue car came in sight and the girls ranged themselves straight across the road so it could not pass until the entire song had been sung. With mouths open ready to sing they stopped in astonishment. The two girls in the tonneau were strangers. They smiled bashfully at the row of maidens with the bright red ties.

Mrs. Bates stepped forward. "Whom have you brought us, John?" she asked.

"Why, you said there'd be two girls in the car when I came out," answered the driver; "and there were."

"Oh, is there any mistake?" asked one of the strange girls. "Our names are Genevieve and Antoinette Rogers. We've come up from Seaville to visit our guardian, Mr. Thurston. He couldn't meet us and another gentleman pointed out his automobile and said the driver would take us out to Mr. Thurston's country place, and we got in, and he brought us here."

"This is Bates Villa," said Mrs. Bates. "You undoubtedly got into our car by mistake."

"I'm sorry this is not the right place," said Antoinette in a tone of frank regret. "I was so glad when I saw all you girls and thought you were to be our friends."

"You will be very welcome guests until your guardian comes for you," said Mrs. Bates in her gracious way.

The Winnebagos were much amused to think that Gladys and Nyoda had missed their chance to ride out in the automobile, and added another verse to the song to be sung when they should arrive on the next Limited. Mrs. Bates found Mr. Thurston's name in the telephone book and called his residence, but could get no answer. Now, Mr. Scovill had introduced himself to Genevieve and Antoinette as "Mr. Adams." They did not know his initials and attempts to get him on the wire were futile.

The girls all went down to the car-track when it was time for the next Limited. A regular fusilade of jests and jibes were prepared for Nyoda and Gladys. The Limited appeared and thundered by without stopping. "Not on this one?" said the girls. "What on earth could have happened?"

"Here comes another car," said Hinpoha; "they're running a double-header. Nyoda and Gladys must be on this one." The second car whizzed by with a deafening clatter and a cloud of dust.

"Maybe they're not coming," said one of the girls, and disappointment was visible on every face. This jolly party would not be complete without their beloved Guardian and Gladys. Mrs. Bates telephoned to the Evans's house in town, but there was nobody home. She tried the house where Nyoda lived, but got no satisfaction, for the landlady merely said that Miss Kent had not been home since leaving for school in the morning. The evening passed off as merrily as possible and the girls rose the next morning feeling sure that Nyoda and Gladys would be out on the first car. But the day passed with no sign of them. They telephoned to the Evans's again and this time they got Mrs. Evans.

"Gladys hasn't arrived there?" she asked in a frightened voice. "She wasn't at home last night. Where can she be?" Wonder gave way to anxiety on all sides and there was no more thought of fun.

"They must be out at Mr. Thurston's, of course," suggested Antoinette Rogers. Renewed efforts were made to get into communication with Mr. Thurston, but in vain. No answer came from the number which was opposite his name in the telephone book. Genevieve and Antoinette were highly embarrassed at being obliged to stay with strangers, and were not a little mystified over the non-appearance of their guardian.

The days passed in frightful suspense for the parents and friends of the missing girls. The aid of the police was called in, but they could find no clue. Early on the morning of the fourth day Mrs. Evans was called to the phone and was overjoyed to hear Gladys's voice on the wire. She and Nyoda were at a house on the lake shore and would be home soon. There was a happy home-coming that morning. Nyoda and Gladys told the almost unbelievable tale of their imprisonment and escape from the tower. After lying exhausted on the beach for a time, they had walked until they came to a house where they were warmed and lent dry clothes, for they had lost their bundles in the waves.

"And that's what would have become of us," said Antoinette Rogers with a shudder, when Nyoda and Gladys had finished their story, "if we had not made a mistake and gotten into the wrong automobile."

The police were informed of the matter and as soon as Mr. Thurston returned to his place of business he was arrested and charged with the conspiracy to abduct and forcibly detain his two wards. At first he denied any knowledge of the affair, but the proof was overwhelming. Nyoda accompanied a delegation of police and witnesses in a motor boat to the foot of the tower and showed them the bent-out bars and the very place where they had jumped into the water, and later they raided the house from the land side. The deaf mute was nowhere to be found. She had fled when she discovered that her charges had escaped and was never heard of again. They ascended in the elevator but were unable to find the contrivance which opened the door into the room, so cunningly was it devised, and had to be content with looking through the grill-work into the lavender room.

The Rogers girls, who were taken away from the guardianship of Mr. Thurston, went to stay with friends in Cincinnati. Mr. Thurston was left to pay the penalty of his villainy alone, for Mr. Scovill had made good his escape before the plot was disclosed.

Thus Nyoda and Gladys all unknowingly were the cause of a great crime being averted, and were regarded as heroines forevermore by the Winnebagos and their friends.

CHAPTER XVII.

JOY BEFORE US.

Aunt Phoebe and Hinpoha, armed with sharp meat knives, were cutting up suet in the kitchen. Hinpoha, as usual, under her aunt's eye, did nothing but make mistakes. "How awkward you are," said Aunt Phoebe impatiently. "You don't know how to do a thing properly. I wish that Camp Fire business of yours would teach you something worth while. Here, let me show you how to cut that suet." She took the knife from Hinpoha's hand and proceeded to demonstrate. The suet was hard, which was the reason Hinpoha had had no success in cutting it, and the knife in Aunt Phoebe's hand slipped and plunged into her wrist. The blood spurted high in the air. Aunt Phoebe screamed, "I'm bleeding to death!"

Hinpoha did not scream. She took a handkerchief and calmly made a tourniquet above the gash, twisting it tight with a lead pencil. Then she telephoned for Dr. Josephy, Aunt Phoebe's physician. He was out. Frantically she tried doctor after doctor, but not a single one was to be had at once. Dr. Hoffman she knew was at the hospital. One of the doctors she had telephoned was said to be making a call on the street where she lived, and she ran down there but he had already left. Running back toward the house, she collided sharply with a man on the street. It was Dr. Hoffman, who was obligingly coming up to deliver a message from Sahwah. "Come quickly," she cried, catching hold of his hand and starting to run, "Aunt Phoebe will bleed to death!"

Dr. Hoffman hurried to the spot and tied up the severed artery. "Who put on de tourniquet?" he asked.

"I did," replied Hinpoha.

"Good vork, good vork," said Dr. Hoffman approvingly, "if it had not ben for dat it vould haf been too late ven I came."

"Where did you learn to do that?" asked Aunt Phoebe.

"Camp Fire First Aid class," replied Hinpoha.

"Humph!" said Aunt Phoebe.

But she did some thinking nevertheless, and was fully aware that it was Hinpoha's prompt action which had saved her from bleeding to death. Her arm was tied up for some days afterward and she was unable to use it. Hinpoha waited on her with angelic patience. "I've changed my mind about this Camp Fire business," said Aunt Phoebe abruptly one day. "There's more sense to it than I thought. If you want to have meetings here I have no objection."

Hinpoha nearly swooned, but managed to say gratefully, "Thank you, Aunt

Phoebe."

Hinpoha began to wonder, as she was thus thrown into closer contact with her aunt, whether Aunt Phoebe's austere tastes came from her having such a narrow nature, or because she had never known anything different. She could not help noticing that there were woefully few friends who came to see her during her indisposition. The daily visit of the doctor was about the only break in the monotony. From a fierce dislike Hinpoha's feelings changed to pity. "I wonder if Aunt Phoebe isn't ever lonesome," she thought. "I don't see how she can help being." A line of her fire song was ringing in her ears:

"Whose hand above this blaze is lifted

Shall be with magic touch engifted

To warm the hearts of lonely mortals——"

"I wonder if I couldn't bring something else into her life," thought Hinpoha. "At least, I'm going to try. Aunt Phoebe's never read anything but religious books all her life. I'd like to read her a corking good story once." Timidly she essayed it. "Wouldn't you like to have me read you something else before we begin the next volume?" she asked, when the third volume conveniently came to an end.

"Do as you like," said Aunt Phoebe, who was profoundly bored. Hinpoha accordingly brought out "The Count of Monte Cristo" which she had been reading when the ban went on fiction, and it was not long before Aunt Phoebe was as excited over the mystery as she was. Romance, long dead in her heart, began to show signs of coming to life.

Hinpoha, looking for a certain little shawl to put around Aunt Phoebe's shoulders one afternoon, opened up the big cedar chest that stood in her room. She had never seen inside of it before. The shawl was not there, but there were quantities of table and bed linens, all elaborately embroidered, and whole sets of undergarments, trimmed with the wonderfully fine crochet work at which Aunt Phoebe was a master hand. "What can all these things be?" wondered Hinpoha. "Aunt Phoebe certainly never uses them." A little further down she came upon a filmy white dress and a veil fastened onto a wreath. Then she knew. This was her aunt's wedding outfit—the garments she had fashioned in her girlhood in preparation for the marriage which was destined never to take place. A week before the wedding the bridegroom-to-be had run away with another girl. The pathos of Aunt Phoebe's blighted romance struck Hinpoha "amidships" as Sahwah would have expressed it, and she wept over the linens in the cedar chest. Poor Aunt Phoebe! No wonder she was sour and crabbed. Hinpoha forgave her all her crossness and tartness of manner, and thought of her only with pity. Her romantic nature thrilled at the thought of the blighted love affair and her aunt became a sort of heroine in her eyes. She yearned to comfort her and make her happy.

Downstairs Aunt Phoebe sat with a letter in her hand. It was from Aunt Grace, Hinpoha's mother's sister, out in California. Aunt Grace had no children and was lonely, and was asking if Hinpoha could come and live with her. Aunt Phoebe pondered. Of late there had been growing on her a conviction that she was not a suitable person to bring up a young girl. She certainly had not succeeded in making her grandniece love her. Aunt Phoebe really was lonely and she did care for Hinpoha, but she did not know how to make her care for her. Her experiment had been a failure. Well, she would send Hinpoha out to California with her Aunt Grace, whom Hinpoha adored, and she would live on by herself. The prospect suddenly seemed rather dismal and she confessed that Hinpoha had been a great deal of company for her, but she would not stand in the way of her happiness. Her mind was made up. She pictured the joy with which Hinpoha would receive the news and it brought her another pang.

At the supper table she told Hinpoha that after school was out she was to go West and live with Aunt Grace, and then sat cynically watching the unbelieving delight which flashed into her face at this announcement. But after the first flush of rapture Hinpoha reconsidered. In her mind's eye she saw Aunt Phoebe living on alone, unloving and unloved, to a lonesome old age. Again she saw the cedar chest with its pathetic wedding garments. Again the words of the fire song came into her mind.

"Do I have to go to Aunt Grace's?" she asked.

"Not unless you want to," said her aunt, wondering.

"Then I think I'd rather stay with you," said Hinpoha.

"Do you really mean it?" asked Aunt Phoebe incredulously. The ice was melting in her heart and something was beginning to sing. Hinpoha slipped out of her chair, and, going around behind Aunt Phoebe, put her arms around her neck. The gate of Aunt Phoebe's heart swung wide open.

Reaching out her arms, she drew Hinpoha down into her lap. "My dear little girl," she said, "my dear little girl!"

And the Desert of Waiting suddenly blossomed with a thousand roses, and Hinpoha saw lying fair before her in the sunlight the City of her Heart's Desire.

Migwan was once more "in the dumps." The heavy strain under which she had been working all winter, coupled with the constant worry and disappointment, produced the inevitable result, and she broke down. She was chosen a Commencement speaker, and the added work of writing a graduating essay was the last straw. She might be able to attend the graduating exercises of her class, said the doctor, but she was not to go to school any more, and of course there was to be no speech prepared. He would not hear of her working in an office during the summer, so her last hope of going to college in the fall went glimmering. But really this last disappointment did not affect her as strongly as the others had done. She was getting used to having everything she touched crumble to dust, and besides, she felt too tired to care which way things went any more.

Thus the month of May brought widely different experiences to the various girls, and went on its way, giving them into the keeping of the Rose Moon. On one of the rarest of rare days that ever a poet dreamed of as belonging to June, the Winnebagos found themselves skimming over the country roads on a Saturday afternoon's frolic. There were three automobile loads altogether, for all the mothers were along, besides Aunt Phoebe and Dr. Hoffman. It was a double occasion for celebration, for besides being the Rose Moon Ceremonial Meeting, it was the day when Sahwah was to lay aside her crutches permanently. The cast had been removed several weeks before and the splintered joint was found to be as good as ever. And Migwan, although she did not know it yet, had more cause to celebrate than all the rest put together. Taken all in all, it would have been hard to find a merrier crowd than that which sped over the smooth yellow road on this perfect summer day, and many a bird, balancing himself on a blossoming twig, ceased his ecstatic outpouring of melody to listen to the blithe chorus of these earth birds, as they sang, "Hey Ho for Merry June," and "Let the Hills and Dales Resound," each machineful trying its best to outdo the others.

And when they came to a sunny hill thickly starred with snowy, golden-hearted daisies they stopped the automobiles and picked great armfuls of the blossoms, and Aunt Phoebe and Dr. Hoffman wandered off by themselves to the other side of the hill in search of larger and finer ones.

Migwan's mother, sitting on the hillside with the warm sweet breeze blowing in her face, felt the joy of health and strength returning with a rush. "Oh," she sighed blissfully to Mrs. Evans, who sat beside her, "I haven't had such a good time since we all went coasting that night. I declare I'm impatient for winter to return, so we can do it again."

"Who says we have to wait for winter before we can go coasting," said Hinpoha, who had overheard the remark. "You just watch this child." Climbing to the top of the hill she beat a path down the slope, and then sat calmly down with her feet stretched out before her and slid down as swiftly as if the hill had been covered with ice. She had no sooner accomplished the feat than all the Winnebagos were at the top of the hill, eager to try it. They came down all in a row, each with her hand on the shoulder of the girl ahead of her, so that it looked like a real toboggan. Then Mrs. Evans tried it, pulling with her stout Mrs. Brewster, who puffed like an engine and got stuck half way down and had to be pushed the rest of the way. Then Dr. Hoffman and Aunt Phoebe returned from their ramble and the mothers hastily collected their dignity and their hairpins, breathless but bubbling over with the fun of it. Whoever has not slid down a grassy hillside in June has certainly missed a joy out of his life.

They had frolicked so long in the daisy field that there was no time to go on to the place where they had intended to cook their supper, and they had to stay right there. Aunt Phoebe had her first taste of camp cookery on this occasion and was delighted beyond words with the experience, as was Doctor Hoffman. "Sometime you and I vill go camping and you vill make someting like dis, mein Liebchen?" he said to Aunt Phoebe, indicating the slumgullion. The group sat petrified at the term he had used in addressing her, and Aunt Phoebe blushed fiery red. Dr. Hoffman saw that the cat was out of the bag. Laughing sheepishly, he spoke. "Dis lady," he said, laying his hand on Aunt Phoebe's, "has promised to be mein vife."

Hinpoha dropped her plate in her surprise. "Aunt Phoebe!" she cried, incredulously, throwing her arms around her. Then her face fell. "You are going away and leave me?" she asked anxiously.

"No, dear," answered Aunt Phoebe, "the Doctor is going to make his home here and we will keep you with us always." And Hinpoha, though still dazed by the news she had just heard, breathed easy again.

When the last bit of slumgullion was eaten and Doctor Hoffman had scraped out the kettle, the Winnebagos retired to the other side of the hill to don their ceremonial costumes, and the rest of the company found comfortable seats on the ground from which to watch the coming performance. As

Migwan was wriggling into her gown a letter fell to the ground. The mail man had handed it to her just as she was starting off with the crowd, and she had thrust it into her blouse to read later. Being dressed a few minutes ahead of the rest, she tore open the envelope while she was waiting for them. If the other girls had been watching her as she read it they would have seen her clasp her hands together suddenly and draw in her breath sharply. Just then Nyoda's clear Wohelo call sounded, and she went with the rest into the circle around the fire.

The Doctor noted with a thrill of artistic pleasure how each girl, as she came over the crest of the hill, stood silhouetted against the red line of the sun for an instant. A ripple of tender amusement went among the watchers as Althea was borne in, clad in her little ceremonial dress and headband.

As this was the big Council Meeting of the year it was more elaborately staged than the ordinary ceremonial meeting. Instead of a large fire being kindled in the center of the circle the first thing, four fires were laid, one in the center and three small ones around it in the form of a triangle. The girls were divided into three groups to represent Work, Health and Love. Each group in turn tried to light the big fire in the center, but in vain; it went out every time. Sorrowfully the groups returned to their own small woodpiles, which they did not think it worth while to light. Suddenly a little, bent old woman appeared from somewhere and stood beside the Work group, shivering with cold. "The stranger is cold," said one of the Work Maidens, "we must light our fire for her sake, even if it is not worth while for ourselves." The fire was lighted and the little old woman stretched out her hands to the cheerful blaze until she was warmed through. Then with a blessing on the Work Maidens she went her way.

Faint with hunger, she stopped beside the Health maidens and begged a bite of food. "We must light our fire and cook something for this hungry stranger," said one of the Health Maidens, "even if it is not worth lighting for ourselves." So they lit their fire and solemnly broiled a wiener which the little old lady devoured eagerly, and passed on, likewise giving them her blessing.

When she came to the Love group it was quite dark, and she begged a light from them that she might find her way up the mountain. So they lit their fire and handed her a torch, upon which she straightened up and threw off her poor cloak and revealed herself as a young and beautiful maiden, the good fairy who inhabited those parts. Holding her torch aloft, she began to dance in and out among the three fires as lightly as a wandering night breeze. Suddenly she stooped to the Health fire and picked up a burning brand; then darting to the Work fire, she picked up a burning brand; then running to the great pile of firewood in the center of the circle, she flung all three down together. The mingled Fires of Work, Health and Love kindled the Fire of Wohelo, which each one separately had failed to light, and as the flames mounted in the big fire the little fires were scattered and stamped out, and the girls sprang to their feet singing, "Burn, Fire, Burn." A round of applause followed this masterly presentation, and Nyoda, who had worked it out, was called on to make a speech. A fine little bit of by-play not planned for by Nyoda was staged when Sahwah dramatically cast her crutches into the Fire of Health.

Now this meeting was the time when the bead-band diaries were to be finished, and the most interesting looking one was to be interpreted if the girl was willing to do so. What tales were worked out in the bands belonging to Migwan, Hinpoha, Sahwah, Gladys and Nyoda! Nyoda hesitated a long time trying to decide which looked the most interesting, Hinpoha's or Migwan's, and finally decided on Migwan's. Nothing loth, Migwan told the story of her hard time during the winter, and the girls in the circle and the visitors alike were stirred by the account of the party dress and the family budget and the returned manuscripts and the vanishing college fund.

"There is one incident not yet recorded," she said, as she came to the end of the figures on the band, "and I really think this ought to be told with the rest." From the beaded pocket of her ceremonial gown she drew the letter which she had read while the girls were dressing. It was from Mrs. Bartlett, the mother of little Raymond, and read as follows:

"To say I was touched to the heart by your story of where the college money went, is putting it mildly. If any one ever put up a brave fight against circumstances, you have. I showed the letter to my husband and he was as much affected as I. And, curiously enough, a letter which we had received earlier in the day, and which had caused us much vexation, contained news of a certain state of affairs which is going to give us a chance to help you out of your difficulty.

"We own a small farm just outside of Cleveland, and for years this has been worked for us by a man and his wife. Just this week this man is leaving our employ to take up some other line of work, leaving the farm without a caretaker at a critical time when the spring vegetables are all up and need attention. Now, our proposition is this: believing that as a Camp Fire Girl you know a great deal about growing things, we are going to ask you to take charge of the place for the summer, and will gladly allow you whatever profit you may make from the sale of vegetables and small fruits if you will see that the peach crop is brought through in good shape and keep the trees from being destroyed by bugs. We will attend to the marketing of the peaches ourselves when the time comes. Good luck to you if you want to undertake the job.

"Your loving friend,

"MABEL E. BARTLETT."

"P.S. We have no objection if you wish to use the house for a Camp Fire

Club House during the summer."

A rousing cheer burst from the group around the fire when they heard this solution of Migwan's problem.

By this time the full moon was climbing over the top of the hill and waking up the sleeping daisies, and the little company rose reluctantly and wandered back to the automobiles that stood by the roadside. Looking back at the peaceful hillside they had just left, it seemed that the nodding daisies and the murmuring brook and the rustling grasses all echoed the song the girls had sung around the fire just before the Council came to a close:

"Darkness behind us,

Peace around us,

Joy before us,

Light, O Light!"

THE END

.

9 781836 574293